Matched with the Small Town Chef

Angel's Peak Steamy Instalove Power Dynamic Novels

Book Four

Ellie Masters

Master of Romantic Suspense

JEM Publishing

This is a work of fiction. While reference might be made to actual historical events or existing locations, the names, characters, businesses, places, and incidents are either the product of the author's imagination or are used fictitiously, and any resemblance to actual persons, living or dead, business establishments, events, or locales is entirely coincidental.

———

DEDICATION

This book is dedicated to my one and only—my amazing and wonderful husband.

Without your care and support, my writing would not have made it this far.

You pushed me when I needed to be pushed.

You supported me when I felt discouraged.

You believed in me when I didn't believe in myself.

If it weren't for you, this book never would have come to life.

ALSO BY ELLIE MASTERS

The LIGHTER SIDE

Ellie Masters is the lighter side of the Jet & Ellie Masters writing duo!
You will find Contemporary Romance, Military Romance,
Romantic Suspense, Billionaire Romance, and Rock Star Romance
in Ellie's Works.

YOU CAN FIND ELLIE'S BOOKS HERE:

ELLIEMASTERS.COM/BOOKS

SUGGESTED READING ORDER

START HERE

Rockstar Romance

The Angel Fire Rock Romance Series

EACH BOOK IN THIS SERIES CAN BE READ AS A STANDALONE
AND IS ABOUT A DIFFERENT COUPLE WITH AN HEA. IT IS
RECOMMENDED THEY ARE READ IN ORDER.

Heart's Insanity

Ashes to New

Heart's Desire

Heart's Collide

Hearts Divided

Hearts Entwined

Forest's FALL

Hearts The Last Beat

CONTINUE HERE...

Military Romance

Guardian Hostage Rescue Specialists

Rescuing Melissa

(Get a FREE copy of Rescuing Melissa

when you join Ellie's Newsletter)

Alpha Team

Rescuing Zoe

Rescuing Moira

Rescuing Eve

Rescuing Lily

Rescuing Jinx

Rescuing Maria

Bravo Team

Rescuing Angie

Rescuing Isabelle

Rescuing Carmen

Rescuing Rosalie

Rescuing Kaye

Cara's Protector

Rescuing Barbi

Charlie Team

Rescuing Rebel

Rescuing Stitch

Rescuing Mia

Jenna's Protector

Rescuing Sophia

Rescuing Malia

Rescuing Ally (Part 1)

Rescuing Ally (Part 2)

Delta Team

Rescuing Ember

Rescuing Aria

STANDALONES IN THE GUARDIAN HOSTAGE RESCUE SERIES YOU CAN READ ANYTIME

Military Romance

Guardian Personal Protection Specialists

Sybil's Protector

Lyra's Protector

Angel Peak Steamy Instalove Novella Series

(Small Town)

By Ellie Masters

EACH BOOK IN THIS SERIES CAN BE READ AS A STANDALONE AND IS ABOUT A DIFFERENT COUPLE WITH AN HEA.

SNOWED IN WITH THE MOUNTAIN DOCTOR

Rescued by the Mountain Guide

Stranded with the Resort Owner

Matched with the Small-Town Chef

Trapped with the Forest Ranger

Snowbound with the Vineyard Owner

Reunited with the Hometown Hero

Colliding with the Coffee Shop Owner

Falling for the Firefighter

Wrecked with the Reclusive Author

Tangled with the Single Dad

Whirlwinded by the Helicopter Pilot

Sheltered by the Veterinarian

Bound by the Sheriff

The One I Want Series

(Small Town, Military Heroes)

By Jet & Ellie Masters

EACH BOOK IN THIS SERIES CAN BE READ AS A STANDALONE
AND IS ABOUT A DIFFERENT COUPLE WITH AN HEA.

Saving Abby

Saving Ariel

Saving Brie

Saving Cate

Saving Dani

Saving Jen

The LaRouge Triplets

Asher

Brody

Cage

Billionaire Romance

Billionaire Boys Club

Hawke

Richard

Contemporary Romance

Cocky Captain

Romantic Suspense

EACH BOOK IS A STANDALONE NOVEL.

The Starling

The Swan

~AND~

Science Fiction

Ellie Masters writing as L.A. Warren

Vendel Rising: a Science Fiction Serialized Novel

————

If you enjoyed this book by Ellie Masters, the LIGHTER SIDE of the Jet & Ellie writing duo, and aren't afraid of edgier writing, you might enjoy reading BDSM themed books written by Jet, the DARKER SIDE of the Masters' Writing Team.

The DARKER SIDE

Jet Masters is the darker side of the Jet & Ellie writing duo!

Romantic Suspense

Changing Roles Series:

THIS SERIES MUST BE READ IN ORDER.

Command Me

Control Me

Collar Me

Embracing FATE

Seizing FATE

Accepting FATE

HOT READS

To My Readers

This book is a work of fiction. It does not exist in the real world and should not be construed as reality. As in most romantic fiction, I've taken liberties. I've compressed the romance into a sliver of time. I've allowed these characters to develop strong bonds of trust over a matter of days.

This does not happen in real life where you, my amazing readers, live. Take more time in your romance and learn who you're giving a piece of your heart to. I urge you to move with caution. Always protect yourself.

Angel's Peak

Grab the First Book in The Guardian Hostage Rescue Specialists Series for Free

https://elliemasters.com/RescuingMelissa

Angel's Peak

Chapter 1

Steamy Encounter

As I climb higher into the Colorado Rockies, the winding mountain road narrows. My rental car hugs curves that grow increasingly tight. A sign announces "Angel's Peak - Elevation 7,623 ft" as pine trees part to reveal a vista so breathtaking it forces me to pull onto a scenic overlook.

Mountains stretch into forever, jagged peaks piercing a sky so deeply blue it seems artificial, like something from a travel brochure promising more than reality could possibly deliver.

But this view *delivers*.

I step out, the thin air immediately filling my lungs with something purer than I've breathed in years. The late afternoon sun ignites the mountainsides, painting them in gold light that will too soon fade. My phone buzzes in my pocket – my editor again, no doubt, demanding updates on a review I haven't even begun. I silence it without looking.

For the next week, I'd love to be just Audrey Tristan, tourist. Not Audrey Tristan, the food critic whose scathing reviews have earned me the industry nickname *"The Executioner."* Not the woman whose takedowns have closed three restaurants in the past year alone. Just a woman on vacation who happens to be writing about her experiences.

That's the lie I tell myself.

Sadly, every bit of that is true.

The thought should bring relief. Instead, my chest tightens with something like dread. When did I become someone who takes more pleasure in destruction than discovery?

The road winds another fifteen minutes before revealing The Haven at Angel's Peak, a sprawling timber and stone lodge that manages to look both imposing and welcoming against its mountain backdrop. Two massive elk antler chandeliers frame the entrance, and somewhere a fire burns, the scent of woodsmoke mingling with pine.

"First time to Angel's Peak?" The valet takes my keys, his flannel shirt, and easy smile part of the carefully cultivated mountain aesthetic.

"Is it that obvious?" My city clothes and pristine luggage might as well be a neon sign.

He chuckles, breath fogging in the cooling air. "We get that look a lot. The first glimpse of the mountains tends to reset something in folks."

Inside, the lobby centers around a stone fireplace large enough to stand in, flames casting dancing shadows across wooden beams and leather furniture. A young woman at reception wears her flannel more formally, with a name tag reading "Emma."

"Welcome to The Haven, Ms. Tristan. We have you in our Mountain View Suite for seven nights." Her fingers fly across the keyboard. "I see you have a reservation for Timberline tomorrow evening as well."

I nod, maintaining the practiced pleasantness that reveals nothing of my purpose. "I've heard wonderful things."

"Chef Morgan creates magic in that kitchen." Pride

brightens her voice. "Anything specific I should note for your dining preferences?"

"No allergies, no restrictions. I'd prefer to experience the chef's vision as intended."

The professional assessment slips out before I can stop it, but Emma just smiles wider. "You're in for a treat."

My room is on the fourth floor, cozy rather than opulent with its king-sized bed draped in a handmade quilt and large windows framing the darkening mountainscape. I unpack methodically – notebook, laptop, the small kit of tools I use to assess portion sizes and temperatures without being obvious. My camera disguised as a casual smartphone. The props of my profession.

Thunder rumbles in the distance. The forecast mentioned afternoon showers, but the speed with which clouds have gathered over the peaks suggests something more substantial brewing. Perfect weather for settling in with room service and research.

But my body aches from hours of driving, and the thought of the walls closing around me after a day confined in the car sends me back downstairs in search of fresh air before the storm hits.

"Any walking paths nearby?" I ask the concierge, a bearded man whose plaid shirt strains slightly across broad shoulders.

"The wildflower meadow trail loops around the property. About a mile total." He points toward French doors at the rear of the lobby. "You'll want to stick close, though. That storm's rolling in fast, and mountain weather doesn't mess around."

The path curves behind the lodge, winding through clusters of aspen trees whose leaves shiver silver in the quickening breeze. The air smells different now – metallic, charged with coming rain. Another rumble, closer this time. I should turn back.

Instead, I follow the path as it forks, curiosity pulling me toward a glass structure gleaming at the edge of the property. A greenhouse, its panels reflecting the churning gray clouds overhead.

The first fat drops of rain begin to fall as I reach the door. It swings open easily, unlocked. Warmth and humidity envelop me immediately, along with the heady perfume of herbs and earth.

This is no ordinary greenhouse – long wooden tables overflow with plants arranged with meticulous care. Herbs I recognize – rosemary, thyme, basil varieties – mingled with edible flowers and vegetables at various stages of growth.

Someone has created an exquisite culinary garden, the kind urban restaurants pay premium prices to maintain. I move deeper into the space, fingers lightly brushing past purple basil, its scent releasing into the humid air. Outside, rain now hammers against the glass, turning the world beyond into a watery blur.

Lightning flashes—an electric slash across the sky. Thunder crashes an instant later, so loud and close it punches through me. I flinch, pulse spiking. The storm is right above us now, turning the greenhouse into a cocoon of trembling glass and humid breath.

"We're not supposed to have visitors back here."

The voice cuts through the air behind me—low, rough, and so close it skates down my spine like the slide of a palm beneath my shirt. I spin, breath caught somewhere between ribs and throat.

He stands framed in the doorway, rain dripping from the edge of the roof behind him. Tall. Too tall for the narrow frame, he ducks slightly as he steps in, his wet shirt clinging to shoulders broad enough to block out half the storm behind him. Dark hair curls damply at his temples. A faint sheen of water slicks his throat. Stubble traces the edge of a jawline sharp enough to draw blood.

But it's his eyes that snare me—clear green-gold, like filtered sunlight through pine needles. Wild. Unsettling. And locked on me with a kind of quiet focus that turns the breath in my lungs to steam.

My mouth moves before my brain can catch up. "I—The door was open. I didn't think anyone— The storm..."

"Caught you off guard?"

The corner of his mouth curves, just barely. That half-smile. Jesus.

"Mountain weather." He moves past me, close enough that I catch the scent of him—rain, earth, something warm and mineral—and my stomach flips. "Zero to sixty in under a minute."

He rolls up his sleeves, slow and efficient. Muscles flex beneath tanned skin as he rinses his hands in the basin, the motion simple, unhurried. Powerful. That body doesn't belong behind a desk. It belongs outdoors. Or pressed against—

I swallow hard, heat blooming low in my abdomen. Get a grip.

I gesture to the rows of vibrant green, trying not to stare at the veins flexing beneath his forearms. "This is... impressive. Do you work for the lodge?"

"Something like that."

He reaches overhead, retrieving a dark bottle and two squat glasses from a shelf above the workbench. His shirt stretches across his back as he moves, rainwater still clinging to him in a way that makes it hard to look away.

"Since neither of us is going anywhere until this passes..." He glances toward the sheets of water blurring the world outside. "Might as well get comfortable. Bourbon?"

I should say no. Should thank him and head back to the lodge with whatever grace I can still gather.

But I nod.

He pours the amber liquid, catching the faint light like wildfire, and his fingers brush mine as he hands me the glass. Barely a touch. But it's enough. A pulse of heat skims along my skin, sinking deep. I pretend not to notice. But I do. God, I do.

"To shelter."

He lifts his glass. I mirror him, and the toast hums between us like a shared secret.

The bourbon goes down like liquid gold—sweet and smoky, and hot enough to make me exhale through my nose. It sears a path down my throat, pooling low. But it's the way he watches me that really sets the fire: over the rim of his glass, eyes half-lidded, the faintest curve to his lips like he already knows exactly what I'm feeling.

No one has looked at me like that in longer than I want to admit. Not with heat and hunger, like this man. Not like I'm a puzzle they want to solve with their hands.

He sets his glass on the workbench, leaning against it. Casual, but every inch of him radiates heat and unspoken strength. His broad chest rises and falls, the damp shirt clinging as if it might never come off.

"What brings you to Angel's Peak?" His voice is low, pulling me back from where my mind's already drifting. "Not exactly on the tourist map."

"Work. Sort of. A working vacation." I grip the glass a little tighter.

The half-truth feels too light for the weight in the air.

"A change of scenery?"

I nod. "From New York. The restaurant scene there is…" I catch myself before I say cutthroat. "Intense."

That glint in his eyes sharpens. A flicker of genuine interest behind the slow-burn flirtation.

"You're in the industry?"

Danger flares hot and immediate—I never reveal my profession to subjects before a review.

"Adjacent," I say, the lie smooth as satin. "Food writing, but not the glamorous kind. Technical stuff."

Another flash cleaves the sky, lightning stark and white, exposing everything. The thunder crashes right on its heels, loud enough to shake the panes. The lights flicker—once, twice—then vanish, plunging us into velvet dark.

"Damn." His voice comes from closer now. My pulse ticks faster. "Backup generator'll kick in for the lodge, but we're on a separate system out here."

"Should we head back?"

The question slips out low and husky. Some small part of me pretends it's concern about the power, but it's not. Not really.

"In this?" His chuckle wraps around my spine like a rope being drawn tight. "Not unless you're craving a complimentary shower. There are worse places to wait out a blackout."

Somewhere above, rain finds a seam in the glass and drums a soft rhythm into the silence—steady, intimate, like a heartbeat.

"I've got a light."

His hand brushes my bare arm as he moves past. Barely a touch, but it sears. Skin-to-skin contact in the dark, and I swear my nerve endings short-circuit.

A soft glow blooms beside me as he flips on his phone flashlight. It casts pale light across his face—that strong jaw, the shadows under his cheekbones, the faint crease at the edge of his mouth as he focuses on the drawer.

"Here we go."

He strikes a match. The sulfur flares, and golden light spills around us as he lights one candle, then another, scattering them across the workbench like stars dropped into our orbit.

The room glows a warm amber, turning the storm into a distant thing, but I don't look away from him—not even when the candles flicker.

His face turns, and he catches me watching. Holds me there. Doesn't flinch. Doesn't pretend.

The air thickens. Charged. Electric in the absence of electricity.

"I don't usually do this." His voice is lower now, scraped raw. It vibrates somewhere under my ribs, in that space behind my breastbone where reason used to live.

"Do what?" My voice barely makes it out.

"Notice someone this fast." He steps closer, and the scent of him hits me—wet earth, bourbon, rain-warmed skin. Something darker underneath. Spiced. Male. Dangerous.

I should move. Should put space between us. Should remember who I am and why I'm here.

But I don't.

Instead, I lift my chin. "I don't usually get noticed."

"Then you've been around blind people." His hand lifts, pausing a breath away from my face. Close enough that I feel the heat radiating off his skin. "May I?"

My yes is barely a breath, swallowed by the silence between us.

His fingers find my cheek—a featherlight stroke, maddening in its restraint. The touch ignites something beneath my skin, a slow burn that spreads like fire through dry grass. Down my neck. Across my chest. Lower.

This is insane.

I don't know his name. Don't know a damn thing except how my body reacts to him—fast, unthinking, molten. Like it's been waiting for this exact touch without knowing it.

Thunder detonates directly overhead, a violent crack that shudders through the glass. I gasp, a cry escaping before I can catch it.

His arms catch me before I can stumble. One hand on my back, the other steadying my upper arm as I collide with his chest—solid, warm, soaked with rain and heat.

We freeze.

My palms flatten against him, feeling the drumbeat of his heart, the slow rise and fall of breath. His hands tighten slightly, not possessive... not yet. But there's a gravitational pull anchoring me to this man like he's the center of some unspoken orbit.

Electricity ripples between us, strong enough to drown out the storm.

His pupils blow wide, swallowing the green.

My gaze drops—to his mouth.

Full. Sensual. The bottom lip slightly fuller, slightly wet.

He's breathing faster now. So am I.

No one knows me here.

Not the version I've built, the perfectly curated mask.

Not the critic. Not the control.

Only this man. Only this moment.

Heat pools low and hard, a pulse between my legs that won't be ignored. My skin aches for pressure. For friction. For him.

His scent curls around me—rain, soil, and bourbon-soaked heat—until I can't think, can't breathe, can't be anything but the desire crawling under my skin.

I slide my hands higher, over his chest, shoulders, until my fingers flex against thick muscle under damp cotton.

His eyes track every movement.

And when I wet my lips—just a flick of tongue across dryness—he watches it like I just stripped off my clothes and asked him to ruin me.

He moves. A breath. A shift. His hands drift from my arms to my back, spreading wide, palms warm as they curve around me.

I arch. Need rising like a tide.

Another rumble of thunder—but this time, I don't flinch. Can't.

I'm pinned by the weight of his attention, by his nearness, by the sheer physical fact of him.

My fingers find the stubble along his jaw, trail upward, tangling in damp hair.

That's what breaks him.

His body goes still—tight with restraint. Then that restraint snaps.

Jaw clenching. Eyes darkening.

And then—his mouth crashes down on mine.

What begins as contact becomes consumption, his lips devouring mine with a hunger that detonates heat low and hard in my belly. I open for him without hesitation, lips parting beneath the insistent press of his tongue. He tastes like bourbon and heat, like the spark of a match catching dry kindling. I burn for him.

The workbench slams into my back as he presses forward, crowding me with the full weight of his body. One hand slides to the base of my skull, anchoring me, the other spanning my lower back and pulling me into him—no space, no breath, no choice but to feel.

His arousal grinds against my stomach, hard and undeniable, and a sound slips from me—needy, involuntary, caught somewhere between a gasp and a moan.

I want more. Want to climb him. Take him. Drown in this.

My hands push beneath the wet cling of his shirt, greedy for bare skin. He's heat and hard muscle, his back flexing as my nails scrape lightly down his spine. He groans into my mouth —a deep, primal sound that vibrates through my chest, matching the thunder still crashing outside.

Then I'm lifted effortlessly as he sets me on the workbench. My thighs fall open, instinctively, aching to bring him closer.

He steps between them, fitting the heavy ridge of his desire right where I throb for him, and my whole body clenches in response.

In the flickering candlelight, his gaze catches mine—no question, no pretense. Just hunger. Just heat.

His fingers thread into my hair, tugging gently to bare my throat. His mouth follows. Teeth graze sensitive skin, dragging a sound from me that feels shamefully raw. I tilt my head back, offering more.

His hand slips beneath my sweater, knuckles grazing my ribs, and I arch into his touch—desperate. When he cups my breast, thumb brushing the already-taut peak, my hips jerk upward with a mind of their own.

He growls, the sound feral. Satisfied. Possessive.

Then his head dips, mouth replacing fingers. The wet flick of his tongue draws a cry from me—sharp and strangled, a sound I didn't know I could make.

Lightning splits the sky, casting us in stark brilliance—my sweater pushed up, his dark head at my breast, my fingers fisted in his shirt like I'll die if he pulls away.

Thunder crashes right on top of it.

My blood pounds so loud it drowns out everything else.

His hands find the button of my jeans. Quick. Sure. Knowing. The zipper follows, sliding down like a promise, and I lift my hips for him, without hesitation. Without thought.

I never do this.

Never lose control.

Never act on impulse. Never surrender to need.

My life is built on restraint, on measured critique, on being the one who watches—never the one who's undone.

But this man. This storm.

This moment that has carved us out from the world...

It's stripped everything else away.

My jeans hit the floor, forgotten. His fingers skim the lace between my thighs, barely touching. Teasing.

The contrast of rough calluses against delicate fabric sends a shiver racing over my skin, every nerve lit like a live wire.

I can't think. Can't breathe.

I only know I want more.

A sound escapes me – half-gasp, half-plea – as he hooks his fingers beneath the thin fabric. He adds my panties to the growing pile on the greenhouse floor.

I reach for his belt, my usually nimble fingers clumsy with urgency. He gently moves my hands aside, making short work of the buckle and buttons beneath. I push impatiently at the denim, needing to feel him, all of him, with an intensity that should frighten me.

When my fingers finally wrap around him, his sharp intake of breath is deeply satisfying – proof that he's as affected by this madness as I am.

The flash of clarity never comes – there's only sensation and need and the overwhelming magnetism between us. He reaches for his wallet without breaking our kiss, handling the issue of protection before returning his full attention to me.

His fingers find me again, testing my readiness. The contact draws another moan from me, my body already embarrassingly eager. His eyes darken as he strokes once, twice, his jaw clenching with barely contained restraint.

I arch against his hand, beyond words, beyond thought. He takes the invitation, positioning himself and driving forward in one powerful thrust that fills me completely.

We both freeze, adjusting to the sensation – the perfect fit, the fullness, the rightness that makes no logical sense but feels like some essential truth my body has always known.

He drives forward in one powerful thrust that fills me

completely, tearing a gasp from my throat. There's no gentleness, no adjustment period – just raw, urgent claiming as his hips snap against mine with an intensity that borders on punishing.

My nails dig into his shoulders as my body arches to take him deeper. Each powerful thrust pushes me closer to the edge, the wooden bench creaking beneath us with the force of our movements. One hand grips my hip hard enough to bruise while the other tangles in my hair, yanking my head back to expose my throat to his mouth.

The workbench creaks beneath us, herbs releasing their scent as we disturb them. Rosemary, basil, something citrusy – a heady backdrop to the more primal scents of rain, sex, and sweat.

He shifts slightly, changing the angle, and suddenly I'm climbing rapidly toward a peak I hadn't expected to reach so quickly. He must feel it in the way I tighten around him, because his movements grow more focused, deliberate. His eyes hold mine, refusing to let me look away as pleasure builds to an almost unbearable intensity.

The tension coils tighter, reaches breaking point. When it snaps, pleasure crashes through me in waves that steal my breath and vision. My cry mingles with another crack of thunder as my body convulses around him.

He follows moments later, his rhythm faltering as he drives deep one final time, body shuddering against mine. For several heartbeats, we remain locked together, his forehead pressed to mine, both of us struggling to catch our breath.

Reality returns slowly. The storm continues around us, but with less fury now, moving past, leaving us in its wake. I become aware of the hardness of the bench beneath me, the cooling sweat on my skin, the absurdity of what we've just done.

He seems to reach the same realization, carefully separating from me and disposing of the condom in a covered bin. We dress in charged silence, stealing glances at each other like teenagers after a first encounter.

"I'm Hunter, by the way." He rebuttons his shirt, a smile playing at the corners of his mouth. "Probably should have mentioned that earlier."

"Audrey." My laughter holds a note of hysteria. "Nice to... meet you."

His gaze drops to my mouth for a beat. Then he steps in close—close enough that his voice can drop into something low and intimate. Just for me.

"Should've told you sooner. But then again..." He leans in, mouth brushing the shell of my ear. "I was enjoying fucking you too much."

My breath stutters. Heat slams into me, all over again.

Before I can recover, he pulls back just enough to meet my eyes, the grin still tugging at his lips—but now there's something darker behind it. Honest.

"Jesus, Audrey..." His voice drops, thick with the echo of what just passed between us. "That was so fucking hot." His gaze flicks to my mouth again, jaw flexing. "You are too fucking hot."

I should say something witty. Clever. Professional.

But I'm still burning. Still bare beneath my clothes.

"Yeah, well..." I lift my chin, voice unsteady but trying for bravado. "You were pretty spectacular yourself."

"Good to know." His grin sharpens, and my pulse skips. "I'm not against round two." He laughs—low and satisfied— like I just confirmed something he already knew.

Round two? Holy granola, I'm not sure if I'll survive round two.

His phone buzzes, the screen lighting up: KITCHEN – Incoming Call.

The spell wavers—but doesn't break.

Hunter glances at it, expression shifting to something more guarded. "Hmm, round two will need to wait. I'm sorry, but I need to take this. The storm probably has things in chaos back at the main building."

"You work at the lodge?" My curiosity piques.

"Something like that." He accepts the call, turning slightly away. "How bad is it?"

The rest of his conversation fades into background noise as I try to compose myself, smoothing down my clothing and running fingers through my tangled hair.

I straighten my clothes, running fingers through tangled hair. The lights flicker once, twice, then hum back to life, exposing the evidence of our encounter – disturbed plants, scattered candles, my flushed face.

"I have to go." Hunter ends his call, already moving toward the door. "Power's back, and I need to do chaos control. Half the staff are stuck in town."

"Of course." Relief floods through me that he hasn't made the connection between random tourist and potential reviewer.

"I hope I'll see you around the lodge?" He pauses at the door, conflict evident in his expression.

"That would be nice."

With a last lingering look, he's gone, disappearing into the now-gentle rain. I give myself five minutes before following, taking the path back to the main building on shaky legs.

My room welcomes me with impersonal comfort – the quilt now turned down, a chocolate on the pillow, the rain pattering against windows that frame mountains now shrouded in mist. I sink onto the edge of the bed, my body still humming with aftershocks of pleasure and adrenaline.

My phone chimes with a notification, shattering the moment of quiet reflection. I reach for it automatically, expecting my editor again.

Instead, it's from the lodge: "Your reservation at Timberline is confirmed for tomorrow at 7:00 PM. Chef Morgan looks forward to preparing a special dining experience for you."

My stomach performs a slow roll that has nothing to do with hunger and everything to do with what just happened in that greenhouse.

I just had mind-blowing sex with a complete stranger.

A stranger, I hope to run into again.

Angel's Peak

CHAPTER 2

PROFESSIONAL SHOCK

THE HOSTESS LEADS ME THROUGH TIMBERLINE'S dining room, her burgundy dress swishing softly against the polished hardwood floors. Exposed wooden beams stretch across the vaulted ceilings, supporting wrought-iron chandeliers that cast a warm, honeyed glow over the space. The scent of cedar mingles with hints of rosemary and thyme, underlining the rustic elegance that permeates every detail.

"Your table, Ms. Evans." She gestures to a prime corner spot beside floor-to-ceiling windows that frame the mountains like living art. Jagged peaks pierce the dusky sky, their snow-capped summits turning rose-gold in the setting sun.

"Thank you." I settle into the buttery leather chair, noting how it's positioned to maximize both the view and privacy. Perfect for a critic who needs to observe without being observed.

The table itself speaks of understated luxury—heavy silverware that catches the light, hand-thrown ceramic plates in earthy blues and greens, linen napkins so crisp they crackle when unfolded. My fingers trace the grain of the wooden table, feeling the natural texture beneath a satin finish.

A server approaches, his movements fluid and unobtrusive. "Welcome to Timberline. May I bring you something to drink while you review our menu?"

"Sparkling water for now, thank you." Professional mode engaged. I've done this hundreds of times, yet anticipation still tightens in my chest. Each new restaurant holds the potential for brilliance or disappointment.

He nods approvingly. "Mr. Reid has spared no expense for this space. The tables were crafted by local artisans from reclaimed timber."

Lodge owner Lucas Reid's reputation precedes him—hospitality mogul turned mountain recluse, pouring millions into this remote property. The investment shows in every detail, from the custom leather chairs to the hand-blown glass light fixtures.

"The chef has created something special here." The server returns with water in a cobalt blue bottle, condensation beading on its surface. "He works exclusively with farms within fifty miles. The microgreens come from our greenhouse."

The greenhouse.

Heat crawls up my neck at the memory of yesterday's encounter. Hunter's calloused hands pinning my wrists above my head against the foggy glass. The urgent press of his body—hard, demanding—as he lifted me, my legs wrapping instinctively around his waist. The way he looked at me, hunger darkening his eyes to midnight, before claiming my mouth like a man starved.

I've never surrendered so completely, never felt so thoroughly possessed by someone whose name I didn't even know.

Six more days in Angel's Peak stretch before me—six days of knowing he's here, somewhere, perhaps thinking about me too.

My body tightens at the thought of another encounter,

another chance to explore this inexplicable chemistry. The way his fingers dug into my hips, possessive and commanding, awakened something primal in me—a curiosity about what it might be like if he stopped holding back, if he took complete control.

If he claimed me entirely.

"Our beef is from Highland Ranch—grass-fed, dry-aged for forty-five days. The mushrooms are foraged from these very mountains by Chef Morgan himself."

I take a sip of water to cool the flush warming my cheeks. "I'll have the chef's tasting menu."

"Excellent choice."

When he departs, I discreetly retrieve my phone, opening the notes app beneath the table. Professional distance. That's what I need now. I came to Angel's Peak to evaluate Timberline, not to dwell on a momentary lapse in judgment with a stranger.

The first course arrives—a delicate amuse-bouche nestled in a spoon carved from mountain stone. Smoked trout mousse topped with trout roe and microgreens. The flavors burst across my tongue—smoky, briny, herbaceous—a perfect encapsulation of mountain and stream.

Two more courses follow, each more impressive than the last. A chilled spring pea soup is poured tableside over compressed apple and mint, and then a perfectly seared scallop, topped with carrot purée and accompanied by brown butter foam. The attention to detail is remarkable, the flavors clean and precise.

I'm midway through the fourth course—elk tartare with pickled ramps and juniper aioli—when a ripple of energy passes through the dining room. Conversations soften, heads turn, and the staff straightens imperceptibly.

The chef has emerged.

He moves from table to table, greeting guests with confidence and warmth. Tall and broad-shouldered in his crisp white jacket, he commands the space effortlessly. Something about his posture, the way he tilts his head while listening to a diner's comments, triggers a flutter of recognition in my chest.

When he turns toward my section, the flutter becomes a stampede.

Hunter.

The man from the greenhouse stands twenty feet away, speaking with an elderly couple at the next table. His dark hair is neatly combed now—no longer mussed by my fingers, no trace of the raw, hungry man who had me spread across a workbench hours ago. His face is composed, professional. Almost indifferent.

But then his gaze finds mine.

Recognition hits like a jolt. A flash of surprise—brief—quickly replaced by something darker. Hungrier.

Like he's remembering the taste of my skin, and the way I sounded when he made me beg.

That look doesn't belong in a dining room. It belongs in the shadows. In bedsheets. In heat.

My breath catches, and I forget how to move.

His pupils dilate, a barely perceptible change from across the room, but one I feel like a physical touch. A hint of a smile touches the corner of his mouth—not the polished one he's been offering other diners, but something private and hungry.

Heat radiates from his gaze as it sweeps slowly down my body and back up, a silent reminder that he knows exactly what I look like beneath my silk blouse. Within seconds, his features smooth into careful neutrality, but the message has been sent. He's found me again, and he's far from disappointed.

My heart hammers against my ribs like a trapped bird. Of

all the restaurants in all the mountain towns in America, I had to walk into his.

He approaches my table with measured steps, as if giving us both time to prepare.

"Welcome to Timberline." His voice carries no hint of our previous encounter, though his knuckles whiten slightly where they grip the back of the empty chair across from me. "I understand this is your first time dining with us, Ms. Tristan."

"Yes, my first time." The double meaning hangs between us, unacknowledged.

"I hope you're enjoying the tasting menu so far." His professional smile doesn't quite reach his eyes, which remain fixed on mine with an intensity that makes my skin prickle with awareness.

"The elk tartare is exceptional." I gesture to my half-finished plate, grateful for something to discuss that isn't the press of his body against mine, the taste of his mouth, the sound of his breathing as it quickened against my ear.

"Thank you. We dry-age the elk loin before preparing the tartare. The juniper berries are gathered on the property."

A server approaches with a question, and Hunter—Chef Morgan—steps slightly away to address it.

The moment gives me space to breathe, to gather my scattered thoughts. Yesterday, I wrapped my legs around this man's waist as he fucked me senseless. Today, I'm evaluating his culinary skills for a review that could make or break his restaurant.

He returns his attention to me. "I'd like to send out something special for your next course. A dish I've been working on that's not yet on the menu."

"That's not necessary." The last thing I need is special treatment that might compromise my objectivity.

"I insist." His tone brooks no argument, though a muscle

ticks in his jaw. "I want to ensure your first experience at Timberline is... memorable."

"It's already been memorable in more ways than one." The words slip out before I can stop them, my voice dropping to ensure only he can hear.

His eyes darken, the professional mask slipping just enough to reveal the man from the greenhouse.

"That's nice to hear." The timbre of his voice changes, deepening to the intimate register that whispered heated promises against my neck. "I had an interesting day myself. Something unexpected. Out of the ordinary." He leans slightly closer, his breath warm against my ear. "Something I hope to taste again."

Heat pools low in my belly, my body responding to his proximity like a tuning fork struck at the perfect frequency.

"I'd like that." No reason to be shy. I gave this man my body before I gave him my name.

When he departs, I drain my water glass, wishing it contained something stronger. The surrounding tables resume their conversations, but I catch fragments about Timberline and its importance to Angel's Peak.

"...saved the town after the ski resort closed..." "...jobs for local farmers..." "...finally putting us on the map..."

The weight of responsibility settles heavily on my shoulders. The Executioner, they call me in industry circles. For my ruthless assessments that have closed more than one ambitious establishment. But those were faceless chefs in anonymous kitchens, not a man whose taste I still carry on my tongue.

The special course arrives—venison loin, perfectly medium-rare, with huckleberry reduction, confit potatoes, and truffle foam. The presentation is a study in controlled elegance, with flavors that are harmonious yet surprising. It's brilliant, innovative cooking that would impress me under any circumstances.

I force myself to analyze it objectively—the technical precision, the balance of flavors, the thoughtful sourcing—but my critical faculties keep stuttering against memories of strong hands, hungry mouths, and a cock that shouldn't be legal.

Desire coils hot and tight, low in my belly. I've never had sex like that. Sex with a stranger. Sex that blew my mind. Sex where I came hard and heady.

The venison remains half-eaten when I signal for the check.

"No dessert, Ms. Tristan?" My server appears concerned.

"Another time, perhaps." I offer a reassuring smile. "A sudden migraine. Please convey my compliments to the chef."

Coward.

But I need space to think, to separate the professional from the personal before I can properly evaluate this meal.

I leave enough cash to cover the bill and a generous tip, then make my escape without looking toward the kitchen. The cool mountain air clears my head somewhat as I stride back to my room, gravel crunching beneath my boots.

The Haven's winding paths are lit by copper lanterns, their flames dancing in the gentle evening breeze. Stars hang impossibly close in the clear mountain sky, brilliant against velvet darkness. Under different circumstances, I might find it romantic.

My room welcomes me with its rustic comfort—patchwork quilt, river-stone fireplace, the faint scent of pine and beeswax. I kick off my boots and collapse onto the bed, staring at the exposed beam ceiling.

What are the odds?

What cosmic joke placed Hunter Morgan's restaurant on my review schedule after placing his body in my arms?

His cock in my...

What am I supposed to do now? Recuse myself? That would mean admitting what happened. Write the review anyway? That would require an objectivity I'm not sure I can muster.

A soft knock at the door interrupts my spiraling thoughts.

"Yes?" I call, not moving from the bed.

"Delivery for Ms. Tristan." A female voice, likely front desk staff.

I drag myself up and open the door to find a young woman holding a cream-colored envelope.

"This was left for you at reception." She hands it over with a professional smile.

Alone again, I turn the envelope in my hands. High-quality paper, weighty and textured. My name is written in a bold, slashing hand. No return address.

The note inside is brief, the ink still slightly damp:

"I need to see you. Meet me at the greenhouse. Midnight. Don't be late. -H."

I press the paper between my fingers, feeling the impression of his pen strokes, the urgency behind them. The command in those five words—"don't be late"—sends a shiver down my spine that has nothing to do with the mountain chill.

He probably wants more free sex. Using me for convenient pleasure while I'm in town.

The thought should offend my professional sensibilities, but instead, it ignites something dark and hungry within me.

No one knows me here. Not really. Not as Audrey Tristan, feared critic who holds restaurateurs' futures in her perfectly manicured hands.

Here, I could be anyone. Do anything. Explore the forbidden corners of desire I've never dared acknowledge in my carefully constructed city life.

Especially with a man like Hunter, who issues commands as naturally as breathing and has them hand-delivered like edicts from on high. A man whose very presence makes me want to yield in ways I never have before.

I should ignore it. Pack my bags. Request a different assignment.

Instead, I reach for my jacket, already knowing I'll go. Midnight suddenly feels too far away.

Angel's Peak

CHAPTER 3

CONFRONTATIONS AND CRAVINGS

THE PATH TO THE GREENHOUSE GLITTERS WITH frost beneath the midnight moon. Each step crunches softly, broadcasting my approach, giving me ample opportunity to turn back.

I shouldn't be here.

Professional ethics demand distance between critic and chef—not midnight rendezvous in secluded greenhouses.

Yet my feet carry me forward, drawn by something beyond rational thought.

The glass structure emerges through the pines, transformed from yesterday's rainy sanctuary into a lantern-lit cavern of secrets.

Dozens of tiny lights hang from the ceiling beams, casting intimate pools of golden light across the verdant space. Steam rises from the heated beds, creating a primordial mist that swirls around the exotic plants.

Hunter stands with his back to the door, white chef's jacket exchanged for a charcoal shirt that stretches across broad shoulders. His dark hair, freed from kitchen constraints, curls slightly at the nape of his neck. The moonlight filtering through glass panels carves his profile in silver and shadow.

He turns at the sound of the door closing behind me. "You came."

"Against my better judgment." My voice sounds steadier than I feel.

The corner of his mouth lifts. "Do you always follow your better judgment?"

"Almost always." The admission feels like surrendering a secret.

He crosses the space between us with unhurried confidence, stopping close enough that I can smell the faint traces of kitchen spices on his skin—cardamom, star anise, something woodsy I can't identify.

"Did you enjoy dinner?" His gaze searches mine, professional curiosity mingled with something darker.

"Yes."

"You left before dessert." His observation contains no accusation, only fact.

Heat crawls up my neck. I don't tell him I was fleeing him, fleeing the confusion his presence stirred in my carefully ordered life.

"I had a headache."

"Convenient." Not believing me for a second. "I saved you something."

He reaches behind him to a small table, retrieving a glass dish that catches the lantern light. Inside sits a perfect quenelle of dark chocolate mousse, topped with gold leaf, beside a sphere of what appears to be passion fruit sorbet. The entire creation is dusted with something that glimmers like crushed stars.

Hunter lifts a small spoon, gathering a perfect bite that combines all elements. "Open."

The command, soft but unmistakable, sends a shiver down my spine. My lips part before my brain can object.

He places the spoon gently in my mouth, his eyes never leaving mine. Flavors explode across my tongue—bittersweet chocolate deepened with espresso, bright tropical passion fruit, and something unexpected—a hint of heat that blooms slowly, building in intensity.

"Ancho chile." The words escape on a breath.

"And Szechuan peppercorn." His thumb brushes my lower lip, catching a stray speck of gold leaf. "Sweet. Hot. Numbing. A contradiction of sensations."

Like the contradiction of wanting a man I barely know, whose restaurant I'm here to judge.

Hunter sets the dish aside, his hand rising to cup my cheek. The gesture should feel tender, but possessiveness radiates from his touch, igniting something primal and hungry within me. His thumb traces my jawline, tipping my face up to his.

"I haven't stopped thinking about yesterday." His voice drops to a register that seems to vibrate through my bones. "About how you felt. How you tasted."

My breath catches. "Hunter—"

"We both know why you're here." His hand slides into my hair, gathering it at the nape with gentle but unmistakable authority. "You wouldn't have come if you didn't want this as badly as I do."

The truth lodges in my throat—he's right, and we both know it.

His mouth claims mine with none of yesterday's hesitation. This isn't the desperate, rain-soaked passion of strangers; it's deliberate, commanding, a man staking his claim. His free hand grips my hip, pulling me roughly against him until nothing separates us but fabric and rapidly deteriorating restraint.

My fingers find the hem of his shirt, desperate for the heat of skin against skin. He breaks the kiss long enough to pull the garment over his head, revealing the terrain of muscle and sinew I explored so frantically yesterday.

In the lantern light, I see what rain and shadows hid—a jagged scar cutting across his ribs, the constellation of freckles dusting his shoulders, the dark trail of hair disappearing beneath his waistband.

My hands drift lower, finding his belt buckle. Our eyes lock as I slowly work the leather free, the metallic clink loud in the humid silence of the greenhouse. The zipper follows, teeth parting beneath my fingers as his breathing deepens.

Something primal and hungry unfurls inside me—a desire I've never voiced aloud, barely acknowledged even to myself.

Without breaking eye contact, I sink to my knees before him, the concrete floor hard against my skin. In my fantasies, I've imagined being put here, but the reality is different—I choose this surrender, and the power in that choice surges through me like electricity.

I free him from the confines of his clothing, taking him in my hand before leaning forward to taste him. A harsh exhale escapes his lips as I take him into my mouth. His fingers thread through my hair, gathering it at the nape in a grip that borders on painful.

"Look at me when you have my cock in your mouth." The command rumbles above me, crude and demanding, his fist tightening in my hair to emphasize his words.

I raise my eyes to find his face transformed with pleasure and something darker—possession, triumph, hunger. His grip yanks sharply when I try to look away, forcing my gaze back to his.

"That's it. Don't look away," he growls, voice thick with arousal. "I want to see those pretty eyes while you take me deep into that mouth."

The raw filth of his words sends heat flooding through me, igniting places his hands haven't even touched. I lose myself in the rhythm he establishes, in the sharp tugs of my hair when I do something he particularly enjoys.

The words send heat flooding through me, my fantasy given voice by his recognition of what this means to me. I lose myself in the rhythm he establishes, in the sharp tugs of my hair when I do something he particularly enjoys.

Without warning, he yanks me upward, strong hands rough under my arms as he pulls me to my feet. His mouth crashes down on mine.

His hands make quick work of my blouse buttons, exposing the black lace beneath. "Better than I remembered." His voice roughens as his fingers trace the edge of the fabric, barely touching skin.

Something shifts in his expression—a darkening, a decision made. His hands close around my wrists, drawing them above my head and pinning them against the door with one large hand. The other traces down my throat, between my breasts, across my stomach to the button of my jeans.

"Don't move."

The command roots me to the spot. He releases my wrists slowly, eyes issuing a silent challenge. My hands remain where he placed them, a voluntary surrender that makes his pupils dilate.

Hunter sinks to his knees before me, his hands working the fastenings of my jeans, sliding them down my legs. Cool air kisses newly exposed skin, raising gooseflesh that his mouth follows with devastating precision. My head falls back against the door, fingers curling against smooth glass as his teeth graze the sensitive flesh of my inner thigh.

"Hunter—please—" The words escape as a gasp.

He rises and reclaims my mouth as he lifts me, my legs wrapping instinctively around his waist. Three strides carry us to a wide wooden table where seedlings would normally germinate. He sets me down, breaking our kiss to look at me —hair wild, lips swollen, chest heaving.

"Turn around."

I comply without hesitation, something electric and dangerous unfurling in my belly at his commanding tone. His chest presses against my back, one arm banding across my collarbone while his lips find the sensitive spot where neck meets shoulder.

"I've been thinking about this all day." His breath caresses my ear. "About bending you over this table and fucking you until you come on my cock. About making you take every inch of me until you can't remember your name. About making you come so hard you see stars."

My legs tremble at his words, at the dark promise they contain. His free hand slides between my thighs, finding evidence of how much his dominance affects me. A groan vibrates through his chest into my back.

"So responsive." Pride colors his voice. "So ready."

The jangling of his belt buckle sends a thrill of anticipation racing along my nerves. My fingers find the edge of the table, gripping tight as denim rustles behind me.

I've never surrendered control so completely, never trusted a virtual stranger with my pleasure, my vulnerability. The realization should terrify me. Instead, it liberates something long suppressed—a desire to be overwhelmed, possessed, to relinquish the constant control that defines my professional life.

His hand at my nape, gentle but firm, bends me forward until my cheek rests against cool wood. "Look at you." Reverence mingles with raw hunger in his voice. "So beautiful like this."

When he finally claims me, the sensation borders on overwhelming—the stretch and fullness, the grip of his fingers on my hips, the sound he makes—half groan, half growl—as he seats himself fully. He remains still for one excruciating moment, allowing us both to adjust to the intensity of the connection.

Then he moves, and coherent thought dissolves into pure sensation. Each thrust drives me higher, his pace merciless yet perfectly calibrated to my responses. One hand leaves my hip to tangle in my hair, pulling just enough to arch my back, changing the angle until spots dance behind my eyelids.

"Look at me." His command pulls my gaze to the glass wall before us, where our reflection shimmers in ghostly outline—his powerful form curved over mine, possessive and commanding. "Watch me fuck you. Watch how your body takes me. I want you to see exactly what I'm doing to you."

His voice drops lower, rougher. "Don't you dare look away. Watch me take you apart. See how beautiful you are when you're desperate for me, getting fucked by me. You don't get to hide from this—from what I'm doing to you, from how much you want it."

The visual combined with his filthy demands pushes me dangerously close to the edge. My reflection stares back at me —flushed, wild-eyed, transformed by pleasure—while behind me, Hunter's powerful body controls every sensation coursing through me.

He must sense it, because his rhythm changes, slows to something torturous. "Not yet."

"Please—" I barely recognize my voice, wrecked and pleading.

His hand slides from my hair to my throat, not squeezing but resting there, a reminder of his control. "When I say."

Time loses meaning as he builds the tension deliberately, bringing me to the precipice again and again without allowing release. My world narrows to his touch, his voice, the inexorable climb toward something that feels like it might destroy me when it finally breaks.

When his fingers find the sensitive bundle of nerves at my center, circling with devastating precision as his thrusts regain their urgency, I can't hold back any longer.

"Hunter, please..."

"Now." His voice, strained with his approaching climax, grants me the permission I didn't know I was waiting for.

Release crashes through me with such force that a scream rips from my throat, my inner muscles clenching around him as wave after wave of pleasure obliterates everything but sensation. He follows moments later, his rhythm faltering as he groans my name against my shoulder, his body shuddering against mine.

For several heartbeats, we remain joined, breath gradually slowing, skin cooling in the humid greenhouse air. His weight presses me into the table, comforting rather than restrictive. When he finally straightens, his hands are gentle on my hips as he helps me turn to face him.

Post-passion vulnerability flickers across his features before his usual confidence reasserts itself.

"Stay here."

He disappears briefly, returning with a damp cloth that he uses with surprising tenderness. The intimacy of the gesture, more than anything that came before, sends heat rushing to my cheeks.

I locate my scattered clothing, dressing with fingers that still tremble slightly. Hunter does the same, though his movements betray none of my lingering shakiness.

"Come with me." He extends his hand. "I want to show you something."

Curiosity overrides post-coital awkwardness. I place my hand in his, allowing him to lead me deeper into the greenhouse to a section cordoned off with humidity controls and specialized lighting.

"These are nearly impossible to cultivate outside their

native environment." Pride infuses his voice as he gestures to delicate plants with spiky purple-tinged leaves. "Alpine thyme. It only grows above eight thousand feet in very specific soil conditions. I've been working with a botanist from the university to recreate those conditions."

His fingers caress the leaves with the same care he'd shown my body moments before. "The flavor is incomparable—more complex than conventional thyme, with hints of pine and citrus. I use it in my venison preparation."

The venison I abandoned half-eaten when I fled the restaurant.

"And these—" He moves to another section, where tiny white flowers bloom on trailing vines. "Wild mountain violets. I crystallize them for dessert garnish."

As he continues the tour, his passion for ingredients becomes evident in every gesture, every carefully chosen word. This is a man who understands flavor on a molecular level, who pursues perfection with single-minded dedication.

The realization lands like a stone in my stomach. I haven't just compromised my professional ethics by sleeping with a chef whose restaurant I'm reviewing—I've done so with a chef whose talent deserves honest assessment, not clouded by personal entanglement.

"You're thinking too loudly." Hunter's voice pulls me from my thoughts. His hand cups my cheek, turning my face to his. "What is it?"

"I've never had a one-night stand." The admission surprises even me. "Let alone a two-night stand, or whatever this is."

"It's called chemistry." A smile tugs at his mouth. "The most powerful kind."

"Not that it can last." Reality intrudes—cold, unwelcome, but necessary. "I'm only here for a week."

His thumb traces my lower lip. "That gives us a week to

enjoy and explore." His eyes darken with suggestion. "There's so much more I want to show you. So many ways I want to have you."

The promise sends a shiver through me, images flashing unbidden—Hunter controlling my pleasure, pushing boundaries I've never dared approach.

"I can't stop thinking about you." The admission costs him something; I see it in the tightening of his jaw. "I haven't been able to focus since yesterday."

"Me neither." More truth than I intended to reveal.

"Stay with me tonight." His request emerges rough-edged, almost vulnerable.

I step back, needing distance to think clearly. "I can't. I have work early tomorrow."

"Of course." Disappointment flashes across his features before understanding replaces it.

The walk to the greenhouse door feels infinite. At the threshold, Hunter catches my hand, pulling me back for one last kiss—gentle now, almost sweet, belying the dominance he'd shown earlier.

"Midnight tomorrow." Not a question. A statement of intent. "Don't be late."

"And if I am?" The question slips out before I can stop it.

Heat simmers in his eyes, turning them almost black in the lantern light. His fingers tighten slightly around my wrist, thumb pressing against my pulse point.

"Best not to find out." The edge in his voice hints at something darker, feeding directly into the fantasy I'm only beginning to acknowledge—the desire to be truly dominated, controlled, to experience whatever consequences he might devise.

Every professional instinct screams for distance, even as my body responds traitorously to his implied threat. The words that slip out of my mouth are completely foreign to me. "As you please...Chef."

"*Fuuuck*," he groans. "Don't do that."

"Why?"

"Because it feeds a part of me you're not ready to handle."

"Don't be so sure about that...*Chef*." I lift on tiptoe to kiss his cheek. "I'll be here, midnight tomorrow, yours to do with as you please."

Before he can respond, I beat a hasty retreat, too heady with the words that just slipped from my lips.

The night air bites at my heated skin as I make my way back to my room, my mind racing with contradictions. The physical evidence of our encounter lingers in pleasantly sore muscles and the phantom impression of his hands on my skin.

My laptop waits on the desk, accusatory in its silent presence. With resignation, I open it, determined to at least make preliminary notes on my dinner at Timberline before tomorrow's breakfast service review.

The email notification chimes as soon as the screen illuminates. From my editor, subject line blunt: "Angel's Peak Assignment."

I click it open, stomach sinking before I even read the words:

"Need your brutally honest take on this one - our readers expect nothing less than your signature takedown if it's warranted. Word is they're gunning for a Michelin star. Your job is to determine if they deserve it. Don't let the mountain charm cloud your judgment. –Margaret"

The words blur as I stare at them, Hunter's taste still on my lips, his touch still imprinted on my skin.

I am so utterly, completely screwed.

Angel's Peak

Chapter 4

Professional Deception

I can't write this.

Not objectively. Not after what we did.

Two nights of mind-bending, hot-as-sin sex with the chef I'm supposed to be evaluating, and now I'm staring at a hotel notepad covered in half-sentences and smeared ink. My notes are useless. My integrity—shattered. My self-control? Left somewhere on a greenhouse floor, tangled in my bra and panties.

The curtains stir with the draft from the window, shadows shifting across the paper like judgment.

I drop the pen, suddenly nauseous. This was supposed to be a job. A review. A quiet escape.

Not this.

Not him.

I need distance. Perspective.

Tossing the notepad aside, I pull on slim-fitting jeans, a cashmere sweater in deep burgundy, and leather ankle boots. The mirror reveals a woman I barely recognize—cheeks flushed, eyes bright with a vitality I haven't felt in years.

This mountain air is having an effect on me. Or, it's not the air at all.

Angel's Peak awaits beyond the Haven's rustic luxury. Time to see what this town is really about.

The main street curves gently around the mountain's base, a postcard-perfect arrangement of storefronts with hand-painted signs and window boxes bursting with late summer blooms. Locals move unhurriedly, pausing to chat on corners, a rhythm of life calibrated to the mountains rather than city deadlines.

Maggie's Diner beckons from the far end—a gleaming chrome-and-red establishment that looks transported directly from 1956. The neon sign hums with electric blue promise, claiming "Best Pie in the Rockies" in sweeping script.

A bell chimes cheerfully above my head as I enter. The aroma hits first—coffee with nutmeg undertones, butter browning on the grill, the sweet perfume of baked fruit and sugar. My critic's nose identifies five distinct pies before I've even spotted them in the rotating display case.

Silence falls like a curtain dropping. Ten pairs of eyes—belonging to men in work-worn flannel, women with weather-lined faces, and a teenager wiping down the counter—all turn to assess the stranger in their midst.

"Take any seat you like, honey." The waitress—sixty-something, with improbably red hair piled high—slides a laminated menu across the counter.

I choose a booth by the window, sliding across vinyl seats that squeak in protest. Condensation beads on stainless steel water pitchers. Silverware gleams under fluorescent lights. Everything is spotless, timeless, and preserved like an exhibit of small-town Americana.

The conversation around me gradually resumes as locals return to their coffee and concerns.

"Haven's brought in three new families this month alone."

A man in a park ranger uniform gestures with his fork. "Twin Pines hasn't seen that kind of interest from outsiders since the mine was operating."

His companion's weathered face, hands spotted with what looks like paint, nods sagely. "It's that restaurant. Timberline's getting write-ups in Denver papers now. The Haven's booked for weddings out for a year."

"Heard they might even get one of those big-city critics coming through." The ranger leans back, hooks a thumb under his belt.

My coffee cup freezes halfway to my lips.

"Lord help us if they get a bad review." The waitress rejoins the conversation, leaning against the counter. "Half the shops on Main only stay afloat because of Haven guests wandering down to browse."

"Morgan wouldn't let that happen. Reid either. Those two are doing everything they can to revitalize this town." The ranger says this with such confidence that something twists in my chest. "Hunter's got more talent in his pinky finger than most chefs have in their whole body. Reid's got his girl pulling in high-profile wedding clients from all across the country... across the globe. Between the two of them, they understand what this place needs."

I lower my gaze to the menu, heat creeping up my neck. The weight of responsibility presses against my ribs. It's not just a restaurant at stake. It's an ecosystem—fragile, interdependent.

Stop it, Audrey.

I've never let sentiment cloud my judgment before.

The readers of Palette depend on my unflinching assessments. My reputation—The Executioner—was earned through brutal honesty, not soft-hearted indulgence for struggling communities clinging to nostalgia and sub-par beignets.

But the coffee tastes different here.

Deeper. Earthier. Like it was roasted over pinewood and memory.

Like the air and the quiet and the man whose fingerprints I can still feel on my skin.

The waitress—Maggie, according to her slightly crooked name tag—sets a plate down in front of me with a conspiratorial smile.

"On the house, first-timer. Can't come to Angel's Peak without trying our berries."

Huckleberry pie. I should be wary—small-town charm rarely translates to exceptional pastry. But the crust gives beneath my fork with the right kind of resistance, crumbling at the edge, still tender at the base.

I take a bite.

The berries explode across my tongue—wild and imperfect and alive. Bright acidity softened by sun and sugar. A crust that tastes of butter and cold hands. A filling that hasn't seen the inside of a measuring cup.

I close my eyes.

The flavor doesn't beg for approval. It just exists. Honest. Undone. Like everything here.

I chew slowly. Swallow. And hate how much I feel.

"That's what I thought." Maggie's laugh is warm and knowing. "Hunter gets his berries from the same patch. My husband's family's been harvesting them for generations."

My professional interest sparks. "For Timberline?"

"Sure. He uses all local stuff. Keeps half this town in business, truth be told." She tops off my coffee. "That boy understands food is about connection. Not just fancy technique."

I manage a noncommittal hum, thumbs moving over my phone screen.

Local sourcing confirmed. Strong community integration. Flavor-forward simplicity.

I add a line under it:

Maggie's deserves a standalone review. Possibly feature column.

I take another bite of pie, and the guilt lands heavier than the fork in my hand. The crust is still warm, the filling just loose enough to bleed slightly at the edges—a balance that shouldn't happen by accident. There's intent in this baking. Heart. History.

Finishing it feels almost illicit.

Every bite pulls me deeper into the fabric of this town— the soft clink of ceramic, the hiss of a stovetop behind the pass, the low murmur of conversations between people who've known each other for decades. It's not just comfort food. It's belonging, served by the slice.

And layered beneath it all, like a wine note I can't un-taste, is him.

Chef Hunter Morgan.

A man who cooks with the kind of control I usually respect, and the kind of raw heat that wrecks me.

I can't stop thinking about his hands—how they plated lamb with surgical precision, and how they dug into my hips like I was his last meal.

After a stroll down mainstream and a short hike along a babbling brook that turns into a quaint mountain stream, I find myself back at The Haven and dinner.

Timberline hums with Friday night energy when I return. I've changed into a simple black dress that hugs my curves without announcing them, paired with understated gold jewelry.

Professional. Detached.

That's my mantra as I enter.

The hostess offers me a table, but I shake my head. "I'll sit at the bar tonight." A better vantage point for observation. Less formal. Less like a critic circling for the kill.

The bartender—bearded, with intelligent eyes behind

wire-rimmed glasses—slides a cocktail menu my way. "First time at Timberline?"

"Second, actually." I scan the room, noting the perfectly timed dance of servers, the sound level indicating happy diners, the way the setting sun gilds everything through the massive windows. "I couldn't stay away."

"That's what they all say." He grins, preparing a gin-based cocktail for another guest. His movements are precise and economical. "Chef's got a way of making sure you come back."

Don't I know it.

I order a glass of local pinot noir from a local vineyard and read the bio about the vineyard.

Silverleaf Vineyards: Angel's Peak's high-altitude terrain creates wines with distinctive character—bright acidity, intense fruit notes, and a complexity that surprises even the most discerning palates. Silverleaf Vineyards sits at 6,500 feet, nestled against the dramatic backdrop of the Rocky Mountains, where the harsh conditions create both exceptional wine and resilient people.

Hunter abides by his locally sourced principles, even in his wines. I'm no sommelier, but this is some of the best wine I've ever tasted.

I swirl the ruby liquid while pretending to check emails. My peripheral vision catalogs everything: the balance of the room, the pacing of courses, the expressions of diners as they taste their first bites.

The kitchen door swings open, and there he is.

Hunter commands his domain with the same intensity he brought to our encounters. A white chef's coat emphasizes the breadth of his shoulders, his dark hair pushed back from his forehead, as his eyes focus on examining a plate before it leaves the pass. Authority radiates from him in palpable waves.

His gaze sweeps the dining room—a captain checking his ship—and locks onto mine.

Recognition. Heat. Challenge.

I don't look away. Can't look away.

He murmurs something to his sous chef and makes his way across the restaurant, navigating between tables with athletic grace. At the same time, my heart performs a complicated gymnastic routine against my ribs.

"Ms. Tristan." He stops beside me, close enough that I catch his scent—rosemary, heat, male. "Returned for another sampling?"

"Professional curiosity." I take a slow sip of wine, letting it linger on my tongue before swallowing. "Your reputation intrigues me."

"My reputation only?" His voice drops low—a private timbre meant only for me. It slides beneath my skin like silk drawn over bare flesh.

The bartender picks up on the shift, retreating down the bar, suddenly obsessed with polishing nonexistent smudges from a row of glasses at the far end.

"I'm very thorough in my research." I trail a fingertip along the rim of my glass, then down the stem, slow and deliberate. His eyes follow the movement like he's imagining my touch on something else entirely. "I like to understand what I'm... consuming."

A muscle in his jaw tightens. Just once. Controlled. But I feel it in my core.

"And your findings so far?" There's an edge beneath the calm, a tension coiled in his tone that thrums between us like a live wire.

"Promising." I meet his gaze, steady. Heat shimmering just beneath the surface. "But inconclusive. I need more... evidence."

He leans against the bar, reducing the space between us by dangerous degrees, slow enough to feel deliberate, close enough that I can smell him: salt, citrus, heat. The space between us shrinks, charged and trembling.

"Well, you have a date at midnight, but if you really want *more*, I'm off Sunday. Let me show you the real Angel's Peak experience."

Professional boundaries scream in warning, howling inside my skull. This is reckless. Dangerous. Delicious.

"I don't think that would be appropriate." But the protest lands weakly between us, laced with want.

"More appropriate than meeting at midnight in my greenhouse?" The corner of his mouth lifts in a half-smile that sends heat spiraling through my core. It lands like a spark in dry brush.

"That was before I knew who you were."

His hand comes to rest on the bar—inches from mine. Not touching. Almost worse. The space between us crackles with restraint.

"And now that you know?" His hand rests on the bar, inches from mine. Not touching. The absence of contact is somehow more intimate than a caress.

I glance at his fingers. Long. Strong. Capable. I remember how they felt inside me. How I came apart around them.

"Now it's complicated."

His gaze dips to my mouth. Stays there.

"It's honest." His eyes darken. "Sunday. Eight AM. I'll pick you up at the lodge entrance."

He straightens, and the loss of his nearness is a physical thing. I grip the stem of my glass tighter to keep from leaning forward.

The look he gives me before turning away is molten.

Not a question. Not a request.

An invitation I already know I'll accept.

My mouth opens to refuse. What emerges is: "Yes, chef."

"You've got to stop doing that."

"Doing what?"

"You know damn well what." He eyes me with heat and hunger.

"Is that so?"

"Yes..." He leans down, whispering in my ear. "Be careful which buttons you push, or you may find yourself in a very compromising position."

My heart just about trips over itself.

"I'll keep that in mind." I could push the conversation, see where it leads, but something tells me to pull back. The lead is not mine to take.

"Enjoy your evening, Ms. Tristan. I'll send over something special." A nod. Satisfaction. He pushes away from the bar, all business again.

I watch him return to the kitchen, heart hammering.

What am I doing?

This isn't just blurring the line between personal and professional—it's erasing it entirely.

The restaurant continues its choreographed ballet around me. Two men at a corner table lean toward each other in serious conversation. One is impeccably dressed in what I recognize as bespoke tailoring—gestures with authority. Lucas Reid, I presume. The lodge owner.

Hunter joins them briefly, shoulders tense under his white coat. The Reid claps him on the shoulder in what appears to be encouragement, but something in Hunter's expression suggests concern beneath his professional mask.

A server delivers an unmarked plate to me—five perfect bites arranged in a geometric pattern that would make a Michelin inspector weep. "Chef's special creation. Not on the menu."

Each bite tells a story of the mountains: smoked trout with foraged ramp custard; venison tartare with juniper and huckleberry; a wild mushroom tart that dissolves on the tongue; alpine herb sorbet that tastes of sunlight on meadows; a miniature chokecherry tart that balances sweetness with untamed tang.

"It's a progression through the seasons of Angel's Peak." The sous chef appears beside me, pride evident as she watches me taste. Mid-thirties, with a sleeve of tattoos visible beneath her rolled-up whites. "Chef Morgan's been working on this concept for months."

I make appreciative noises, professional critique momentarily forgotten in pure gustatory pleasure.

"This place means everything to him," she continues, eyes following her boss as he expedites at the pass. "To all of us, really. The Haven might look like a rich man's playground, but for locals, Timberline represents hope. Economic survival."

She's gone before I can respond, called back to her station by some kitchen urgency.

I observe Hunter through new eyes as the evening progresses. The way he coaches a young line cook through a mistake rather than berating him. His insistence on personally inspecting dishes for a customer with severe allergies. The respect—not fear—his staff shows him.

This isn't just a chef building a reputation. This is a man building a community.

By the time I leave, my notebook is filled with observations that have nothing to do with food execution and everything to do with the man behind the cuisine. Dangerous territory for a critic known for her objectivity.

The greenhouse glows with soft amber light when I arrive at midnight, as instructed in his text. Condensation beads on glass walls, creating a dreamlike veil between this space and the real world.

Hunter stands between rows of exotic herbs, sleeves rolled to his elbows, forearms corded with muscle as he transplants seedlings. He doesn't look up at my entrance.

"You're on time." His voice carries in the humid air.

"I'm always punctual for appointments." I move toward him, drawn by forces I still can't name. "Professional habit."

"Is that what this is? Professional?" He finally raises his eyes to mine, intensity burning away pretense.

"Nothing about this is professional." My admission hangs between us.

In three strides, he's before me. No words. No preamble. His mouth claims mine with devastating precision, tasting of mint and man and unchecked hunger.

My body responds instantly, molten heat pooling low in my belly. I grasp his shoulders, fingertips digging into hard muscle as he walks me backward until I feel the edge of a wooden table against my thighs.

"I've been thinking about this all night." His words rumble against my throat as he trails fire down my neck. "Watching you at that bar, pretending we're strangers."

"We are strangers." I gasp as his teeth graze my collarbone.

His laugh is dark, knowing. "Your body doesn't think so."

He lifts me onto the table, stepping between my thighs. My dress rides up, his hands find bare skin, and all coherent thought evaporates in the greenhouse heat.

There's none of the tenderness of our first encounter. None of the exploration of our second. This is raw need, primal and demanding. Claiming and being claimed.

When it's over, we're both breathing hard, skin damp with exertion and the humid air. Reality filters back slowly. What I've done. What I'm still doing.

"Sunday." He tucks a strand of hair behind my ear, the gentle gesture at odds with the fierce possession of moments before. "Eight AM."

I climb down from the table on shaky legs, adjusting my clothing with as much dignity as possible. "This can't happen again."

"It already has. Three times." He steps back, giving me space.

"I'm establishing boundaries." I move toward the door.

"Too late for that." His smile isn't unkind. "We're way past boundaries. Or, rather, it's time to start exploring what boundaries we each have."

I have no response because he's right. We're in uncharted territory now.

"As you wish."

Back in my room, I shower away the evidence of our encounter but not the memory. Opening my laptop, I stare at the blank document that should contain my preliminary notes on Timberline.

The cursor blinks accusingly.

What exactly are you going to say, Audrey?

That the chef has magic hands in more ways than one? That you can't trust your judgment because you're sleeping with the subject of your review?

A ping from my phone interrupts my self-flagellation. A text from my editor: "Found something interesting about your mountain chef."

My stomach drops as I click the link. The screen fills with an article from three years ago—the dramatic closure of an upscale Denver restaurant. Bankruptcy. Lawsuits from investors. And at the center of it all, a promising young chef named Hunter Morgan.

The accompanying message makes my blood run cold: "Look familiar? Think there's a pattern with our mountain chef?"

I stare at Hunter's younger face in the article photo, wondering exactly what I've gotten myself into—and what secrets he's keeping behind those intense eyes that seem to see right through my professional deception.

Angel's Peak

CHAPTER 5

MOUNTAIN REVELATIONS

THE WOODEN LODGE ENTRANCE GLOWS AMBER IN the early morning light as I check my watch for the third time in five minutes. Seven fifty-eight. My breath puffs visible in the mountain chill, dissipating into nothing against the cloudless blue sky.

I'm nervous.

Not the calculated tension before conducting a critical review, but something fluttery and adolescent that I haven't felt in years.

A forest-green Jeep Wrangler with mud-spattered sides rounds the corner precisely at eight. Hunter sits behind the wheel, sunglasses reflecting the morning light, his profile sharp against the mountain backdrop. My heart performs an embarrassing little skip.

He steps out, dressed in worn hiking boots, jeans that hug his muscular thighs, and a flannel shirt with sleeves rolled to expose corded forearms. So different from the commanding chef in whites, yet equally magnetic.

"Morning." He takes in my outfit—premium hiking pants,

merino wool top, and boots that have never seen actual dirt. "You'll do."

"I wasn't aware there was a dress code." I slide into the passenger seat, catching the scent of pine and coffee.

"For where we're going, there is." He hands me a thermos. "Black, one sugar. Right?"

The fact that he's noticed how I take my coffee sends an unwelcome warmth through my chest.

"Should I be concerned about your plans?" I unscrew the cap, inhaling the rich aroma.

"Scared?" His eyebrow arches above his sunglasses.

"Cautious." I take a sip, the coffee is perfect. "I'm not exactly the outdoorsy type."

"City girl through and through?" The Jeep rumbles to life, engine vibrating beneath us.

"New York for the last decade." No need to mention the dozens of other cities I've visited for reviews. "Concrete and taxis are more my natural habitat."

His laugh is unexpected, genuine. "Then you're in for an education."

We climb steadily along winding mountain roads, the Haven growing smaller in the side mirror. Hunter drives with the easy confidence of someone who knows every curve and dip intimately. His hands rest loosely on the wheel, strong and capable.

The same hands that explored my body last night. Heat rises to my cheeks at the memory.

"First stop." He pulls into a graveled overlook where a wooden sign proclaims, "Lookout Point - Elevation 8,743 ft."

The view steals my breath more effectively than the altitude. The valley spreads below us in a tapestry of emerald forest and silver ribbons of water, framed by jagged peaks still wearing patches of snow despite the summer season.

"Best view in the county." A ranger in a tan uniform approaches, clipboard in hand. "Morning, Hunter."

"Steve." Hunter nods in greeting. "Conditions good today?"

"Clear through early afternoon. We're expecting a front to move in around two." The ranger checks his watch. "Make sure you're down by then. Weather changes fast up here."

"Always does." Hunter turns to me. "Steve's grandfather taught mine how to track elk through these mountains."

"Been here long?" I ask, curiosity about Hunter's past overriding my professional detachment.

"Seven generations." Hunter's voice carries pride. "My family helped found Angel's Peak when the railroad came through."

This connection to place and history is foreign to me. My rootless existence—moving from city to city, restaurant to restaurant—suddenly seems hollow by comparison.

We leave the ranger and drive higher, eventually turning onto a dirt road barely wider than the Jeep itself. When even this peters out, Hunter parks beneath a massive pine.

"From here, we walk." He retrieves a backpack from behind his seat. "You good with that?"

"Lead the way." I adjust my ponytail, oddly determined to prove I'm not some helpless urbanite.

The trail is narrow, climbing through stands of aspen whose leaves shimmer like coins in the morning light. Hunter moves with the sureness of someone following a path etched in memory, rather than one marked on the earth.

We stop at a small clearing where the ground is carpeted with tiny white flowers. Hunter kneels, examining them with reverent fingers.

"Alpine strawberry. Impossible to cultivate commercially." He picks one and offers it to me. "Taste."

The berry is warm from the sun, bursting with an intensity that makes commercially grown varieties taste like pale imitations.

"This is what food should be." His voice drops, passionate. "Experienced in its place, at its peak moment of perfection."

He fills a small cloth bag with berries, explaining each plant we encounter, which are edible, which are medicinal, which are sacred to the indigenous people who first inhabited these mountains.

We discover a patch of morel mushrooms nestled in the shadow of a fallen log. Hunter's hands move as he harvests them, leaving enough to spread their spores.

"I come here every spring. Never tell anyone the location." He glances up at me. "You're the first person I've brought."

The significance of this admission settles between us, weighted with intimacy that has nothing to do with our physical encounters.

"Why me?" The question escapes before I can reconsider.

He stands, morels carefully stowed in his pack. "Because you understand the language of food. I could see it in your eyes when you tasted that first dish at Timberline. You get it."

Guilt squeezes my chest. Would he be so open if he knew my real purpose here?

The path narrows as we continue higher, wildflowers dotting the alpine meadows in explosive bursts of color. Hunter points out edible plants—wild onion, mountain sorrel, tiny sprigs of thyme growing improbably from rocky crevices.

We round a bend and freeze. Twenty yards ahead, a massive bull moose raises his enormous rack, regarding us with suspicious eyes.

"Don't move." Hunter's body shifts imperceptibly, positioning himself between me and the animal.

The moose snorts, pawing the ground. My heart hammers against my ribs. The creature is magnificent and terrifying—all muscle and wild intention, completely beyond human control.

Slowly, deliberately, Hunter raises his arms to appear larger, never breaking eye contact with the moose. "Back up. Very slowly."

I inch backward, hyperaware of every twig and stone beneath my boots. The moose watches, deciding.

After an eternity compressed into seconds, the animal turns away, ambling into the forest with surprising grace for something so massive.

My breath releases in a rush. "That was—"

"Close." Hunter's arm remains extended protectively in front of me, his body a shield. Only when the moose disappears does he lower it, but he stays close, scanning the trees.

Something shifts inside me at this instinctive protectiveness. This isn't the calculated charm of men who've pursued me in the past—restaurant owners seeking favorable reviews, chefs looking to leverage my connections. This is primal, unthinking. Real.

"Thank you." I touch his arm, feeling muscle still tensed beneath flannel.

"Bull moose in rut don't mess around." His eyes soften as they find mine. "You okay?"

"Better than okay." And I mean it.

Adrenaline courses through me, every sense heightened. I feel more alive than I have in years of dining at the world's finest restaurants.

The sky darkens abruptly as we make our way back down the mountain, clouds gathering with alarming speed above the peaks. Wind whips through the trees, temperature dropping noticeably with each gust.

"Steve wasn't kidding about that weather front." Hunter glances at his watch, concern creasing his brow. "We need to move faster."

The first fat raindrops hit as we cross an exposed ridge, quickly intensifying to a driving sheet that reduces visibility to mere yards. Thunder cracks overhead, too close for comfort.

"The Jeep's too far." Hunter takes my hand, grip firm. "One of Jackson Hart's cabins is just over that rise. We can wait it out there."

We half-run, half-slide down a muddy path I wouldn't have noticed without him. The temperature plummets as hail begins mixing with the rain, stinging exposed skin.

The cabin materializes through the downpour—a basic stone structure with a small covered porch. Hunter retrieves a key from beneath a hollowed log that says 'Key HERE,' and ushers me inside.

"Hiker's shelter. He has several scattered around the mountains." He shuts the door against the howling wind. "Basic, but it'll keep us alive."

The interior is smaller than my bathroom at the Haven—a single cot, a tiny wood stove, and shelves stocked with emergency supplies. Hunter moves, searching the shelves. He finds what he's looking for and strikes a match to kindling already laid in the stove.

"Who's Jackson Hart?" I wrap my arms around myself, shivering as the adrenaline fades.

"Local legend. Built these shelters all over the mountain after his fiancée died in an accident." Hunter feeds small logs into the growing flame. "There's a change of clothes in that trunk. Nothing fancy, but they're dry."

The trunk yields thick wool socks, flannel shirts, and thermal leggings that smell of cedar. I turn my back to change, suddenly shy despite our previous intimacy.

The stove gradually warms the small space, our wet clothes steaming on a makeshift line strung across one corner. Outside, the storm rages with increasing fury, hail replaced by snow that shouldn't be falling this early in September.

"We could be here a while." Hunter sits on the edge of the cot, leaving space for me. "Might as well get comfortable."

Angel's Peak

Chapter 6

Ten Things and One Confession

I join him, the cot creaking beneath our combined weight. "Is this your idea of the real Angel's Peak experience?"

"Not quite how I planned it." His chuckle rumbles through the small space. "But authentic, nonetheless. Mountain weather waits for no one."

Silence stretches between us, filled with the crackle of the fire and the howling wind. This strange intimacy—trapped together, wearing borrowed clothes, isolated from the world—feels more exposing than our physical encounters.

"I expected you to pounce the moment we were alone in here." The words escape before I can filter them.

His eyes meet mine, amusement mixed with something darker. "Is that what you think this is about? Just sex?"

Heat floods my cheeks. "Our previous encounters suggest a certain... pattern."

"Maybe I want to know the woman I've been having mind-blowing sex with." He shifts to face me more fully. "Let's play a game. Ten things."

"A game?" I raise an eyebrow.

"Ten things we have in common. I'll start." He leans back against the wall. "I hate cilantro. Tastes like soap."

A startled laugh escapes me. "It does. Everyone thinks I'm crazy when I say that."

"Genetic trait. About twenty percent of the population has it." He gestures for me to continue. "Your turn."

"I can't whistle." I demonstrate my pathetic attempt, producing only a rush of air.

"Neither can I." He tries, failing spectacularly. "Drove my grandfather crazy. He could whistle any tune perfectly."

"Your grandfather?" The mention of family snags my interest.

"He raised me after my parents died. Car accident when I was seven." His voice holds old pain, long since accommodated but never truly healed. "He was the cook at the old Angel's Peak Hotel before it burned down. Taught me everything I know about food."

"Is that why Timberline is so important to you?" I ask, forgetting momentarily that I'm supposed to be hiding my professional interest.

His eyes sharpen, but he answers. "Partly. It's his legacy as much as mine." He pauses, weighing something. "Also my redemption."

"From what?"

The stove pops loudly, sending a shower of sparks against the grate.

"I had a restaurant in Denver. Very high-end, molecular gastronomy stuff. Investors, magazine features, the works." His jaw tightens. "My business partner decided he wanted full control. Sabotaged equipment, stole recipes, spread rumors to suppliers. By the time I figured out what was happening, the restaurant was bankrupt and my reputation was trash."

The article my editor sent flashes in my mind. There's always more to the story.

"That's why Lucas gave me Timberline. He was one of the few who didn't believe the rumors." Hunter's fingers trace patterns on the rough wool blanket. "He's not just my friend —he's betting his entire lodge on me. The Haven is operating on thin margins, staying afloat mainly because of the restaurant."

Guilt claws at my insides. The weight of my pending review feels suddenly crushing.

"Your turn." He nudges my knee with his. "Something else we have in common."

We continue the game, discovering shared traits both trivial and significant. We both sleep on the left side of the bed. Both lost a parent too young. Both prefer savory to sweet. Both feel most at peace in the hour before dawn.

"Last one." I've shifted closer during our exchange, drawn to his warmth. "I'm terrified of disappointing people who believe in me."

His eyes hold mine—unflinching, open. There's something raw behind them, something recognizing and wounded, like he's let me see a part of him no one else does.

"That makes ten."

Outside, the storm still claws at the cabin walls, but inside, the atmosphere has shifted. Heavier. Deeper. No longer lust, no longer just escape.

"I have a confession," I blurt, the words pulled from me like breath from lungs.

His hand comes up, cupping my cheek with devastating gentleness. The rough pad of his thumb brushes over my lower lip—slow, deliberate, anchoring me in sensation.

"Confess to me."

The invitation curls in the air between us. And somehow, it's enough to make me drop every mask.

"I like it when you take charge." My voice is low, but it

trembles. Not from fear—from truth. "It turns me on when you... control things."

His smile is quiet. Dangerous. Tender.

"Part of taking charge," he murmurs, lips ghosting across mine, "is knowing when to go slow..." A kiss. Barely there. "...and when to heat things up."

I swallow hard. "If you had full control... what would you do to me?"

That stillness returns—the kind that prickles across my skin, anticipatory and thick. When he speaks, his voice is velvet wrapped around steel.

"First, I'd bind your hands. Nothing fancy—just enough to make you feel helpless."

My breath hitches.

"Then," he continues, brushing hair back from my face, "I'd strip you slowly. One piece at a time. I'd make you stand there and take it—let you feel every second of being exposed just for me."

My thighs press together involuntarily. He notices. Of course he does.

"Then I'd test you." His hand slides to the curve of my neck. "A few soft taps of my hand. Just enough to make you gasp. Then a little harder. Just enough to make you wonder how much more you can take." His mouth moves to my ear. "I'd put you on your knees. Not because you had to—but because you'd want to. Because you'd ache to serve me."

A shudder moves through me so violently that I nearly collapse against him.

"I want that." The words break out of me, desperate. "I want you to do that to me."

His next kiss is slow and possessive, a claiming made of breath and heat and restraint. No rush. No hunger without patience. Just the promise of what's to come.

When his hands finally slide beneath the flannel, it's not

with urgency—but with reverence. Like he's unwrapping something sacred.

The cot creaks beneath us as we shift, adjust, and explore.

A new rhythm. A new hunger.

My body arches into his touch as he learns me again—not just to possess, but to command. To know.

And I let him. Because for the first time in my life...sex feels like freedom.

His mouth moves down my neck—not kissing so much as claiming, the heat of his breath drawing goosebumps across my skin.

"Lie back," he murmurs.

I obey.

The cot creaks beneath me as I sink into it, heart pounding so loudly I'm sure he hears it. My hands tremble as they rest by my sides, but I don't hide it. I don't want to.

Hunter stands over me, eyes raking down my body like he's mentally mapping where he'll touch first.

"Do you trust me?"

The question lands like a stone in a still lake—rippling, reverberating.

"Yes."

That's all he needs.

He takes off his belt slowly—not for shock, not for show —just purpose. Precision. He threads the leather between his fingers, then kneels beside the cot.

"Hands up." His voice is soft, but unyielding.

I lift my arms, breath catching as he wraps the belt around my wrists. Not tight. Just firm. Restrained. His fingers are careful as he tugs it snug, testing the resistance, watching my face the entire time.

"Too much?"

"No." My voice breaks, needy.

"Not enough."

The smile he gives me is pure fire.

He raises my bound hands over my head, securing them to the bedframe with a strip of flannel torn from his own shirt. Improvised. Personal. Intimate. When he leans over me, the muscles of his arms bracket my body, and his mouth hovers just above mine.

"Now you don't get to touch until I say."

He strips me slowly, reverently—each button undone like a secret whispered only to him. The flannel peels away, revealing skin already flushed, aching.

"You look better like this," he murmurs, trailing fingers down my sternum. "Open. Exposed. Waiting."

My hips lift without thinking, searching for friction, for contact.

He presses one hand to my thigh to still me, eyes narrowing with quiet command.

I still. I burn.

He trails kisses down my torso, lingering at my hip, my belly, each touch a slow dismantling of my control.

Then he sits back on his heels and—with deliberate ceremony—runs a single fingertip up the inside of my thigh.

"Now I'm going to test you." His voice is low. Serious. "Not to hurt you. But to show you what you can take. What you want to take."

I nod—breathless, helpless.

"Please."

His hand lifts.

The first slap lands soft—barely a sting. More sound than sensation. But it makes me gasp.

"Good girl."

A second one—firmer. Just enough to spark heat beneath the surface.

"Let me hear you."

I moan—shocked by the sound that escapes me. Raw. Honest. His.

"That's it."

He rewards the sound with his mouth between my thighs, slow and devastating.

I arch, bound and exposed and completely at his mercy.

"Stay still." His voice strokes across my skin like velvet over flame. Not raised, not rushed—just absolute. My wrists tug reflexively against the belt binding them to the frame, but I obey. "You don't move unless I say."

His fingers skim the inside of my thigh again, a whisper of touch that leaves me straining for more. But nothing comes.

Nothing... and everything.

Because that's the game now—he controls the pace, the pleasure, the torment of waiting.

"Breathe for me."

I do. Inhale. Exhale. Shaky. Loud. Aroused beyond reason.

Hunter watches me—not just my body, but the way I react to the absence of sensation. The way I arch into empty air. The way I clench around nothing.

"Good girl."

Two words. They land harder than his hands.

He leans in close, breath warm against my ear.

"I'm going to use you exactly how I want. And you're going to take it. Because that's what you need, isn't it?"

I nod, breathless. Desperate.

His hand closes around my jaw, firm but careful, angling my face toward him.

"Words, Audrey."

"Yes." I choke on the word. "Please."

A growl rumbles in his chest—satisfaction and hunger, restrained only by discipline. He moves with calm efficiency, pushing my legs wider, adjusting my hips, and then... stepping away.

The loss of him steals the air from my lungs.

"Hunter—"

"When we're like this, you don't speak unless I ask you a question." His tone sharpens—still quiet, but no longer soft.

I go still. The shame is instant... and so is the heat.

He watches the war play out across my face. His gaze darkens, but there's pride in it too. He sees me. All of me.

And I want to give him everything.

He moves back between my thighs, brushing his knuckles along my soaked panties.

"You're trembling." He smiles faintly. "Perfect."

He peels the fabric down agonizingly slow, lips following the motion, kissing the path he exposes. Then his mouth is on me again—not gentle this time, but claiming. Ruthless.

I cry out. Hands straining against the belt. Back arching. Body unraveling.

"Stay down," he murmurs, not even looking up. "Take it. All of it."

I try. God, I try.

But it's too much—his tongue, his fingers, the weight of being owned in this moment.

"Hunter—please—I can't—"

He looks up now, mouth wet with me, eyes alight with heat and power.

"Yes, you can." His voice is steel wrapped in silk. "I decide when you come. Not you."

He returns to his task like a man starving. Every flick of his tongue is deliberate. Every sound he pulls from me is absorbed with purpose. Controlled chaos beneath his hands.

And when he finally slides two fingers inside me, curling them in just the right way, I nearly scream.

"That's it," he murmurs. "Let me break you open."

Angel's Peak

CHAPTER 7

SAY PLEASE

HUNTER'S MOUTH IS A WEAPON. HE USED IT TO drive me higher and higher—expert, merciless, devastating. The pleasure builds in sharp, shattering waves, like something alive clawing up my spine. My thighs tremble against his shoulders, the bindings at my wrists cutting delicious tension through my arms.

I'm right there. So close it's agony.

"Please," I gasp. "Please, Hunter—let me—"

He pulls back just enough to speak, lips brushing slick heat.

"You want to come?" His voice is ruined velvet. "Say it."

"Yes—God, yes—please let me come, I need it—"

His eyes meet mine—dark, commanding, utterly in control.

"Then come for me, Audrey."

A beat.

"Now."

The permission detonates inside me.

My body convulses. Shudders. Breaks.

Sound tears from my throat, raw and unfiltered. My hips

buck against his mouth as he keeps working me through it, relentless and reverent all at once.

He doesn't stop until I'm shaking, breathless, wrecked, and trembling in my restraints.

When he finally rises, he looks like a god made of sweat and hunger—his jaw tight, his chest rising with barely contained need.

"That's mine," he says softly, eyes dragging down my limp, sated form.

"That noise. That face. That surrender. All of it—mine."

He rises slowly, eyes raking over my wrecked, limp form, wrists still bound, chest rising and falling in uneven bursts.

But he's not done.

Not even close.

He unties the belt from the bedframe, then steps back, pulling me upright with a grip on the restraints still wrapped around my wrists.

"On your knees."

The words land like a lightning strike. No hesitation. No question.

Just command.

My body moves before thought can interfere. He guides me down, not rough, but firm, sure. Claiming. The wooden floor is cold beneath my knees, grounding me, making the ache between my legs feel even more raw, even more real.

Hunter stands above me, unbuttoning his jeans with slow, deliberate fingers.

His eyes never leave mine.

"You offered yourself to me." He strokes himself once—long, slow, the head flushed and hard. "Now you show me what that means."

My mouth opens, eager, but he grips my chin—thumb pressing into the hinge of my jaw, holding me still.

"No rushing. No control. This is mine." His thumb

brushes my lower lip, smearing the taste of myself across it. "Open."

I obey.

He slides in slowly, letting me feel the weight of it—the stretch, the heat, the power of the moment. His hand stays on my jaw, guiding, controlling, but not choking.

Not yet.

His hips move in a shallow rhythm, letting me adjust. Letting me serve.

"Eyes on me," he growls when I start to close them. "I want to see how much you love this."

I moan around him. My knees press into the floor. My bound wrists hang between us, helpless, offered.

He groans, head falling back for one stolen second—then he's looking down again, gaze dark and blistering.

"Fuck, Audrey... you were made for this."

His control slips just a fraction. He starts to thrust, deeper now, hand fisting in my hair, holding me exactly where he wants me. I take it. All of it. The rhythm. The fullness. The complete, unquestionable domination.

"You don't get to stop," he pants. "Not until I come. Not until I give you what I need."

Tears prick the corners of my eyes—not from pain, but from overwhelming pleasure, from the sheer act of surrender.

I hollow my cheeks, moaning around him, tongue working him as best I can. He tightens his grip, pace faltering —and I feel it—his loss of control.

"Fuck—Audrey—"

He thrusts once, twice—then stills. Buries himself deep.

The groan he lets out is feral, his release thick and hot and claiming.

When he finally pulls back, his breath drags ragged and uneven through his chest. He gathers me against him like something precious, his palm splayed across my spine, the weight of his touch grounding and deliberate. I melt into it, into him, the scent of sex and rain and smoke wrapping around us like the storm outside.

I should feel raw. Hollowed out. But instead, I feel powerful—remade. Not from being taken, but from the way I gave myself over completely and he never once let me fall.

He kisses me again, slow and reverent this time, and I think maybe that's the end. Maybe we'll lie here, tangled and breathless, warm and sated until the storm passes.

But the belt is still tight around my wrists, and when I lift them toward him in a silent question—will you untie me now?—his gaze drops, lips curling into something dark and wicked. That smile does more to my insides than the orgasms combined.

"You think we're done?" His voice is rough silk, a low rasp that scrapes across every nerve ending with delicious friction. "You don't get to decide when this ends, Audrey. That's not how giving up control works."

I should've known. I did know. But hearing it from him, watching that heat spark back to life in his eyes as he wraps a fist around the belt between my bound wrists and pulls me upright—it makes me throb all over again.

"You're mine until I say otherwise."

The cot creaks under his weight as he shifts behind me, and before I can even catch my breath, he's moving. Positioning me. Knees hitting the edge of the mattress. Bound hands pulled behind my back. His grip tightens just enough to remind me he's still in charge, even as he eases me down until my chest presses to the mattress and my ass tilts up for him, completely exposed.

He doesn't ask if I want it. He doesn't need to.

He knows. My soaked thighs, my parted lips, my shattered moans already gave me away.

"You begged so pretty with my cock in your mouth," he

growls behind me, the heat of his body pressing close as his fingers trail up my inner thigh, deliberately skirting where I need him most. "Let's see how well you beg when I fuck you from behind."

He doesn't give me time to answer. One sharp thrust and he's inside me again—so deep, so sudden it punches the air from my lungs. I cry out, but it's not pain. It's need. Pure, blinding need as he drags back and slams into me again, setting a brutal rhythm designed to break me open all over again.

One hand fisted in my hair, the other gripping my bound wrists as leverage, he fucks me like he's staking a claim, every stroke hitting deep, angled, unrelenting. I can't do anything but take it—mouth open, gasping, legs trembling with the effort to stay upright as pleasure coils dangerously low in my belly, tighter and tighter until it borders on pain.

"You come when I say," he growls, teeth grazing the shell of my ear as he leans over me, the weight of him pressing me down. "You hold it. You fucking hold it for me."

I sob into the mattress, my whole body shaking with the effort, the denial excruciating and exquisite. He never lets up. Just keeps pounding into me, dragging me higher, edging me closer, whispering filth in my ear until I'm incoherent with need.

"I feel you clenching around me. You're so close. But you don't come without my permission. Not until I'm ready to feel you fall apart again."

My scream gets muffled by the pillow when he slaps my ass, the sting blooming fast and hot, followed by the dizzying rush of arousal that spikes so hard I nearly black out.

He leans back, lets go of my wrists to wrap one hand around my throat, pulling me upright, impaling me deeper onto him. My bound hands are pinned between us, my thighs slick, trembling, stretched wide to take him. I want to scream. I want to cry. I want to come so badly I can taste it.

"Now," he says, voice guttural and savage. "Come for me now."

I explode. Body convulsing. Hips jerking. Muscles clamping down around him like a vice. I come so hard I sob with it, collapse forward, barely aware of his grunt behind me as he follows me over the edge, spilling inside me with a shudder that rocks the bed.

But he's not done.

He doesn't pull out. Doesn't soften.

His hand fists in my hair again, dragging my head back as he mutters, "One more."

I barely have time to breathe before he flips me over, rips my thighs apart, and slides back inside, still hard, still ravenous. He fucks me through my oversensitivity, through the whimpers and gasps and tears that spill down my cheeks, claiming every inch of me all over again.

And I take it.

All of it.

Because he's in control. I gave that to him.

He's still buried inside me when his hand smooths up my spine, slow and open-palmed, not a command this time, but a comfort. A question lingers in the air, heavy as the scent of sweat and sex clinging to our skin.

"Was that too much?" His voice comes rough, low, barely audible beneath the thunder.

My breath catches, not from what he did to me, but from the fact that he'd ask. That, after all that taking, he still wants to be sure I enjoyed it, too.

I lift my head, meeting his eyes in the dim light. There's no teasing now. No smirk. Just raw honesty, waiting in the soft line of his mouth.

"It was perfect." I shake my head slowly.

And I mean it. My body aches in the best way—used, marked, sated—but beneath the wreckage, there's peace. A kind of bone-deep rightness I didn't know I was starving for until he gave it to me.

The storm provides our soundtrack—wild and untamed beyond the walls, while something equally powerful but infinitely more tender unfolds within.

Afterward, tangled in scratchy wool blankets on the too-small cot, I rest my head on his chest, listening to his heartbeat slow. This feels dangerously like intimacy beyond the physical —the kind that leaves marks no one can see but that never truly fade.

His hand finds the curve of my hip under the covers, thumb stroking idly, grounding me in this quiet aftermath. I don't want to move. Don't want to speak. I just want to memorize the rhythm of his breath beneath my cheek.

"The storm's passing," Hunter murmurs, voice vibrating under my ear. He turns his head, glancing toward the window.

Sure enough, the wind has calmed, though snow continues to fall in fat, wet flakes that won't stick but transform the landscape into something magical.

"I wish we could stay like this forever." I swallow. The words come before I can weigh them.

A beat. The silence stretches between us. Then—

"Me too..." His arms tighten around me. "Me too."

We dress in our now-dry clothes and make our way down the mountain. The forest glistens, every surface adorned with melting snow that catches light like scattered diamonds.

The Jeep, thankfully, starts on the first try. We descend toward town, where Hunter insists we stop at the farmers' market occupying the town square every Sunday.

The scene could be from another century—wooden stalls laden with fresh produce, handmade goods, and local specialties. Hunter moves through the crowd, greeted by name at every turn.

"Morgan, just in time." An elderly woman waves from

behind a display of honey jars. "Saved you the last of the meadowfoam. Knew you'd be by."

"Mrs. Winters." Hunter kisses her weathered cheek. "You're a saint."

He introduces me to what feels like the entire population of Angel's Peak—the blacksmith who forges his custom knives, the cheese maker whose aged cheddar features in Timberline's signature soufflé, the retired schoolteacher who supplies rare heirloom tomatoes from her greenhouse.

These aren't just suppliers. They're his extended family, a community bound together by food and shared history.

"Last stop." Hunter leads me to a stall selling hand-knitted items. "Emily's mittens will change your life."

The shy teenage girl behind the table blushes when Hunter compliments her work. I select a pair in deep burgundy, warmed by the simple joy on her face when I compliment her craftsmanship.

Snow begins falling again as we walk back to the Jeep, transforming the town into a picture-perfect postcard. Lights glow from shop windows, smoke curls from chimneys, and the mountains stand like sentinels in the background.

For one suspended moment, I allow myself to imagine belonging to a place like this.

To him.

"Thank you for today." I mean it more deeply than he can know. "I've never experienced anything like it."

His eyes hold mine, snowflakes catching in his dark lashes. "There's a lot more to show you. If you want..." The promise in his voice extends beyond geography.

"I'd like that." That's when it hits me with crystal clarity—I'm falling for him.

For this place.

For a life I've never even considered possible.

The realization terrifies me more than the moose, more

than the storm, more than anything I've faced in years of ruthless professional detachment.

Back in my lodge room, I peel off layers of mountain-scented clothing and step into a steaming shower. Today revealed Hunter in ways our previous encounters never could.

The chef is impressive, but the man—connected to his community, passionate about his home, protective and patient—is something else entirely.

How can I possibly write an objective review now?

My phone rings just as I wrap myself in the Haven's plush robe. My editor's name flashes on the screen.

"Audrey, Glad I caught you." His voice bursts through the speaker, New York energy jarring against the mountain peace. "I need a draft of your review in three days. This one's going on the cover."

My stomach plummets. "The cover?"

"'Mountain Miracle or Rustic Disappointment?'" He sounds gleeful. "Your takedown of that pretentious Seattle place boosted our subscriptions by fifteen percent. Readers are expecting something equally brutal or breathlessly admiring. Either way, we need click-worthy content."

"I'm still gathering impressions." My voice sounds distant to my own ears.

"Well, gather faster. Three days, Audrey. Make it juicy."

The call ends, leaving me staring at my reflection in the steamy mirror. *The Executioner.* That's who they want.

But the woman who spent the day in Hunter Morgan's mountains, who learned his secrets and shared her own, who's falling for a man and a place she was only supposed to judge—she wants something else entirely.

Angel's Peak

CHAPTER 8

KITCHEN CONFIDENTIAL

THE TEXT MESSAGE ARRIVES AS I'M HALFWAY through my second cup of coffee, curled in the window seat of my lodge room, watching early morning mist rise from the mountains.

"Timberline's closed Mondays. Private cooking lesson? 4pm."

My fingers hover over the screen. This is crossing yet another line in a rapidly disappearing professional boundary.

A food critic doesn't take cooking lessons from her subject. She doesn't spend days exploring his hometown. She certainly doesn't sleep with him repeatedly, and she absolutely *never* allows him to bind her hands and take control during sex.

The Executioner would never.

But Audrey—the woman who felt something crack open inside her on that mountain yesterday—types back: *"I'll be there."*

Research.

That's my paper-thin justification as I select a casual and flattering outfit—dark jeans that hug my curves and a soft cashmere sweater in deep forest green. I tell myself the extra time spent on my makeup and hair is merely a professional presentation.

The lies I tell myself are becoming more elaborate by the day.

Timberline looks different in the afternoon light—softer, more intimate, without the evening bustle.

The "CLOSED" sign hangs on the door but swings open at my touch. The dining room sits in hushed expectation, chairs inverted atop tables, sunlight streaming through the massive windows painting golden patterns across the hardwood floors.

"Back here." Hunter's voice calls from the kitchen.

I follow the sound, my heels clicking against the polished concrete floors of the back hallway. The professional kitchen gleams with stainless steel precision, knives aligned on magnetic strips, and copper pots hanging in size order above a massive range.

Hunter stands at a central prep island, a white apron tied over a simple black t-shirt that stretches across his shoulders. His forearms flex as he fillets a fish with hypnotic efficiency, each movement precise and controlled.

"You came." He glances up, a smile warming his features.

"I was intrigued." I set my purse on a stool, suddenly aware of how out of place my city-self appears in this temple of culinary creation. "Though I should warn you—my cooking skills are limited to reheating takeout."

"Perfect." His grin widens. "Blank slate. No bad habits to unlearn."

He washes his hands, dries them on a towel tucked into his apron, and approaches. When he leans in to kiss me, it feels natural, as if we've been doing this for years rather than days. His lips taste faintly of something herbal and bright—he's been tasting as he works.

"My grandfather's special mountain trout." He gestures to the pristine fillets. "Caught this morning by Hank Turner up at Crystal Lake. Still swimming at dawn."

The fish gleams pearlescent under the professional lighting, its flesh the pale pink of sunrise. Next to it, small piles of ingredients wait in precise grouping—fresh herbs, mushrooms, tiny potatoes with soil still clinging to their skins.

"First rule of cooking—*mise en place.*" He hands me an apron. "Everything in its place before you begin."

The apron smells of laundry soap and faintly of him. I tie it around my waist, ready to play student to his teacher.

"We'll start with the herbs." He guides me to a cutting board. "Hold the knife like this."

His hand covers mine, adjusting my grip on the chef's knife. His chest presses against my back, warm and solid. This position is ostensibly instructional, but the brush of his breath against my ear suggests other intentions.

"Rock the blade, don't chop." He demonstrates, our hands moving in unison. "Let the knife do the work."

The herbs release their fragrance as we cut—thyme, dill, chervil—creating an aromatic cloud that tingles in my nose and clings to my fingers. When he steps away to check something on the stove, I feel the absence of his heat like a sudden chill.

"What's next?" I ask, oddly proud of my neatly minced herbs.

"Mushrooms." He places a basket of tiny golden chanterelles before me. "These grow on the north side of Widow's Peak. I harvested them last week."

I learn to clean them with a small brush rather than water and slice them to preserve their delicate texture. Hunter moves around the kitchen with the grace of a dancer, effortlessly reaching for ingredients and adjusting the heat, all while maintaining a running commentary on his grandfather's techniques.

"He believed food should taste of place." Hunter measures out a splash of amber liquid. "This is local honey mead. The Johnsons have kept bees here for four generations."

Everything connects to story, to history, to the mountains surrounding us. This isn't cooking as I've experienced it in the world's top restaurants—technical, competitive, designed to impress. This is cooking as communion with place, with memory, with legacy.

"Taste." He holds out a spoon with a small amount of sauce, his other hand cupped beneath to catch any drips.

I lean forward, lips parting. The flavor blooms across my tongue—butter richness balanced with herbal brightness and the subtle sweetness of the mead. My eyes close involuntarily.

"Good?" His voice has dropped half an octave.

"Incredible." I open my eyes to find him watching me with intense focus.

"Your turn." He hands me the wooden spoon. "Stir while I prep the garnish."

We move around each other in the spacious kitchen. He shows me how to test the potatoes with the tip of a knife, how to crisp the trout skin to a perfect golden brown, and how to plate with an artist's eye for composition.

"Final touch." He reaches past me for a jar of vibrant orange roe. "Wild steelhead caviar from the river that runs through town."

With tweezers, he places tiny dots of the glistening eggs around our plates. The completed dishes look like edible land-scapes—the trout nestled on herb-flecked potatoes, surrounded by golden mushrooms, and the bright pops of roe. Sauce is swirled like a mountain stream around the perimeter.

"Beautiful." I'm genuinely impressed by the dish and how much I've enjoyed creating it.

Without thinking, I pull out my phone, capturing the perfect composition from several angles. The light catches the glistening trout skin, the vibrant orange roe, and the delicate herbs—a masterpiece that deserves documentation.

"For your memory collection?" Hunter asks, looking pleased by my appreciation.

"Something like that." I take one final shot that captures the dish with the mountains visible through the window behind it—place and plate in perfect harmony.

"Not done yet." Hunter disappears into the wine room, returning with a dust-covered bottle. "2010 Kistler Chardonnay. Been saving it for a special occasion."

He uncorks the bottle, pouring golden liquid into crystal stems that catch the late afternoon light streaming through the windows.

"To your first Timberline creation." He raises his glass.

We carry our plates and wine to a small chef's table in the corner of the kitchen—an intimate space where the staff might taste new dishes or hold meetings.

The first bite nearly brings tears to my eyes. Not because of technical perfection, though it has that in abundance. But because I can taste the mountain streams, the forest floor, and the history of this place in every mouthful.

This is what I've been missing in all those sterile, perfect restaurants I've eviscerated in print.

Soul.

Connection.

Purpose beyond accolades.

"You're quiet." Hunter watches me over the rim of his wineglass.

"It's perfect." The words feel inadequate. "I've eaten in the best restaurants in the world, and this is..." I stop, realizing my mistake.

His eyebrow lifts. "You've eaten in the best restaurants in the world?"

Heat floods my face. "I mean, when I can. For special occasions." The lie tastes bitter compared to the perfect food on my plate.

He accepts this with a nod, but something flickers in his eyes—doubt, perhaps. I change the subject quickly.

"Tell me more about your grandfather. He taught you to make this dish?"

The tension dissipates as Hunter shares stories of his childhood in these mountains, learning to forage and fish alongside the old man who raised him. As the sun sets beyond the windows, we finish the wine, and Hunter clears our plates despite my offer to help.

"Guest privilege." He stacks them in the industrial dishwasher. "Besides, I like watching you enjoy the view."

I stand at the massive windows, watching Alpenglow—a beautiful optical phenomenon that paints the mountaintops in shades of pink and gold opposite the sun. The beauty of this place still takes me aback. It is so different from my usual urban haunts, with their concrete and neon signs.

"Thank you for coming today." Strong arms wrap around my waist from behind, and Hunter's lips find the sensitive spot below my ear.

"Thank you for inviting me." I lean against his chest, allowing myself this moment of perfect contentment.

"I have ulterior motives." His hands slide beneath the hem of my sweater, warm against my skin.

"Do you?" I turn in his arms, finding his eyes darkened with intent.

"I've been thinking about you in my kitchen since you walked in." His thumb traces my lower lip. "The way you looked, concentrating on cutting those herbs. The little sound you made when you tasted the sauce."

Heat pools low in my belly, desire flaring quickly after the slow burn of our cooking session. My hands find the solid planes of his chest through his t-shirt.

"Thinking about me, how, exactly?" My voice emerges huskier than intended.

Instead of answering, he lifts me in one fluid motion, setting me on the edge of the prep table. His mouth claims mine with a hunger that has nothing to do with food, tongue teasing, teeth grazing my lower lip in a way that draws a gasp from deep in my throat.

My legs wrap around his waist, pulling him closer. The kitchen, with its gleaming surfaces and precise tools, recedes into the background, reduced to a backdrop for this consuming need that's built between us.

"Here?" I manage between kisses, my hands already working at his belt.

"Here." His voice holds absolute certainty. "I want to remember you in this kitchen long after you're gone. I want to know I fucked you here."

The words pierce through the haze of desire—a reminder that my time in Angel's Peak has a definite endpoint. That none of this is meant to last.

I push the thought away, focusing instead on the feel of his hands pushing my sweater up and over my head, the cool air of the kitchen against my heated skin, the contrast of the cold stainless steel at my back, and his burning touch at my front.

He takes his time despite the urgency of our need, removing each piece of clothing with deliberate care and kissing newly exposed skin with reverent attention. By the time we're both naked, I'm trembling with anticipation, past coherent thought, or professional concern.

The passion that ignites between us feels different than our previous encounters—deeper, laden with emotions neither of us has voiced. His hands and mouth map my body as if committing it to memory. I arch against him, nails scoring his back as he brings me to the edge again and again before finally joining our bodies.

We move together on that stainless steel altar to food, creating something equally primal and nourishing. Each release tears through me with an intensity that leaves me gasping his name, and clinging to his shoulders as if he's the only solid thing in a world turned liquid with pleasure.

Afterward, he wraps me in his chef's coat, the fabric warm and smelling of him. We end up on the floor, backs against the prep island, limbs tangled together in sated exhaustion.

"I'm falling for you." He speaks the words into my hair, voice rough with emotion. "I know it's fast. I know it's crazy. But there it is."

My heart constricts painfully in my chest. I should tell him now. Who I am. Why I'm here. Before this goes any further.

Before more damage is done.

Instead, I kiss him, pouring everything I can't say into the press of my lips against his. The embers of our earlier passion reignite instantly. I push him back against the floor, straddling his hips in one fluid movement.

"Again?" His eyes darken and his hands find my waist.

I answer by rolling my hips against his, feeling him hardening beneath me. Taking control feels like reclaiming some small piece of agency in this web of deception I've spun around us both.

My hands press against his chest, pinning him as I set the rhythm. His chef's coat falls open around me as I move, my skin flushed and hypersensitive.

I want to burn this moment into memory—the way he looks up at me, desire and something deeper darkening his eyes, the way his hands grip my thighs hard enough to leave marks, the way my body knows exactly how to take what it needs from his.

When release comes this time, it's with my head thrown back, his name a breathless prayer on my lips. He follows immediately, the tension in his body snapping as he pulls me down against his chest, our hearts racing in thunderous counterpoint.

When we finally dress and restore the kitchen to its immaculate state, twilight has deepened into true night. Hunter pours a small glass of whiskey as a nightcap.

"To unexpected connections." He touches his glass to mine.

As I sip the smoky liquid, my gaze wanders to the wall near his office. Framed reviews hang in a neat row—some glowing with praise, others blistering with criticism. One particularly savage takedown bears a byline I recognize— Julian Marsh, the San Francisco Chronicle's notoriously vicious critic.

"Battle scars." Hunter notices my attention. "Some fair, some not."

"Do reviews matter that much?" I ask, guilt churning beneath casual curiosity.

"More than they should." He traces the condensation on his glass. "Especially now. Lucas is feeling the pressure from his investors. The Haven isn't turning the profit they expected. Timberline is doing well, but not well enough to carry the whole operation."

He stares into his whiskey, something vulnerable crossing his features. "A major positive review could change everything. Bring in the clientele who stay in the premium suites, not just dine at the restaurant."

The weight of my deception presses on my chest, making breathing difficult. Every day I don't tell him the truth makes the eventual revelation more damaging.

"Several publications have approached us." He continues, unaware of my internal struggle. "Lucas is particularly hoping for coverage in Palette. Their reviews can make or break a place like this."

"Palette?" My glass nearly slips from my suddenly nerveless fingers.

"Yeah. They're known for having the toughest critic in the business—some woman they call 'The Executioner.' Her take-downs are legendary." He shakes his head. "Though honestly, I'd rather face her than lose this place. Angel's Peak needs Timberline. These people—" he gestures toward the town beyond the windows, "—they're counting on us."

"I should go." I set my glass down, gathering my purse with hands that want to tremble.

"Everything okay?" Confusion clouds his expression.

"Just tired." The lie comes easily now, one more in an expanding collection. "And I have work to catch up on."

"I'll walk you back to the lodge."

"No need." I move toward the door, desperate to escape before my face betrays me. "I could use the fresh air to clear my head."

His brow furrows at my sudden withdrawal, but he doesn't press. "Call me when you get in?"

"Of course." I force a smile that feels like it might shatter my face.

When I exit, the night air hits like a slap, the mountain chill cutting through my emotional turmoil. Stars wheel over-head, indifferent to the human drama unfolding beneath them.

I walk rapidly back to the Haven, my mind a hurricane of competing thoughts. The truth of what's happening is unavoidable now.

I'm falling in love with the subject of my review. A review that could save or destroy everything he's built. Everything this town depends on.

The Executioner wouldn't hesitate.

She'd write an objective assessment regardless of personal entanglements. That's her brand. Her professional identity.

But I'm not sure I can be her anymore. Not after seeing Hunter in his element. Not after understanding what Timberline means to this community. Not after feeling something I've never felt before in his arms.

In my room, I open my laptop and create two documents. The first contains the truth—a glowing review of Timberline's innovative approach to mountain cuisine, its deep connection to place, and the technical skill behind dishes that sing with authenticity.

I upload the photos of the trout dish we created together. They're the perfect visual evidence of what makes this place special—not just technical perfection, but soul and connection to the land.

The second is what my readers expect—a clever, cutting assessment that finds fault with pretension, questioning whether mountain ingredients can genuinely compete with coastal abundance, and wondering if the chef's personal history has made him too safe, too rooted in tradition.

Both contain enough truth to be defensible. Both would satisfy my editor's demand for "click-worthy content."

My finger hovers over the send button on both drafts. Who do I want to be?

The Executioner. Or the woman I'm becoming in Hunter Morgan's mountains.

I've never had trouble making this choice before.

Angel's Peak

Chapter 9

Community Connections

Morning light spills across my laptop, where both drafts of my review remain unsent. I've barely slept, the weight of my decision pressing against my chest like a physical thing. Professional integrity versus something I barely recognize in myself—this unfamiliar yearning for connection, for belonging.

The walls of my luxury suite at The Haven suddenly feel confining. I need air. Perspective. Distance from both Hunter and my own tangled thoughts.

I dress quickly in jeans and a light sweater, grabbing my jacket to ward off the mountain morning chill. The lobby is quiet, with only a single staff member polishing the already gleaming reception desk.

"Heading into town?" His name tag reads "Jeffrey," and his smile seems genuinely warm rather than the practiced hospitality smile I've grown accustomed to in luxury establishments.

"Yes. Any recommendations?"

"Maggie's has the best breakfast, but you might try The Pickaxe for lunch. It's the only real bar in town. Best burgers in the county." He leans across the desk conspiratorially. "Don't tell Maggie I said that."

The path into Angel's Peak has become familiar now—past the stone marker commemorating the town's founding, down the gentle slope where pines give way to the first weathered buildings. Mid-morning sunshine gilds everything in honey light, the mountains standing like sentinels in the background.

Angel's Peak looks different today. No longer a picturesque backdrop for my review, but a living community with heartbeats and histories. People nod as I pass, a tentative acknowledgment that I'm becoming a recognized face rather than just another transient tourist.

The Pickaxe sits at the far end of Main Street, a squat building of rough-hewn logs with a faded wooden sign depicting crossed mining tools. It looks like it's been standing since the town's founding, worn smooth by time and use.

A bell jingles as I push open the heavy wooden door. The interior is dim after the bright mountain sunshine, smelling of beer, old wood, and something delicious simmering from the kitchen. A massive stone fireplace dominates one wall, currently cold in the summer heat. Vintage mining implements and black-and-white photographs cover every available surface.

The bar runs the length of the room, polished to a high shine by generations of elbows. Behind it, bottles glint in the light filtering through small windows. A handful of locals occupy scattered tables despite the early hour, conversations dropping to curious silence as I enter.

I approach the bar, where a woman in her sixties, with steel-gray hair pulled into a severe bun, regards me with a frank assessment.

"What can I get you?" Her voice has the rasp of either cigarettes or hard living.

"Whatever's on tap and the burger I've heard about." I slide onto a stool, aware of eyes watching from corner tables.

She pours a golden ale from a tap marked with a hand-carved wooden sign reading "Angel's Tears." The beer arrives in a heavy glass mug, condensation already beading on the sides.

"Haven guest?" she asks, punching my order into an ancient register.

"Yes. Audrey Tristan." I offer my name as a small concession, an opening.

"Ruth Fletcher. My family's owned this place since 1912." She gestures to a faded photograph behind the bar showing a much younger version of the building. "Back when this was a proper mining town."

The ale is surprisingly complex, with notes of pine and citrus balanced by a smooth maltiness. I comment on this, earning a slight softening around Ruth's eyes.

"My nephew's brewery. Started in his garage five years ago. Now he supplies half the restaurants in three counties." She wipes an already clean section of bar. "Including your chef friend's place up at The Haven."

The possessive warms me despite myself. "Hunter seems committed to sourcing locally."

"Saved more than a few businesses around here doing that." This comes from a man at a corner table, white-haired and weathered as the mountains themselves. "When the mine closed in '89, this town nearly died. Tourism's all we got now."

A plate appears before me—a burger that makes a mockery of the gourmet versions I've critiqued in Manhattan steakhouses. Hand-formed patty on a house-made brioche bun, melted cheese that stretches when I lift the top, handcut fries still glistening from the fryer.

"Morgan designed this burger for us." Ruth's voice carries

unexpected pride. "Taught my cook how to grind the right blend of cuts, how to season it proper."

I take a bite and close my eyes. It's the perfect ratio of fat to lean, seasoned with a hand that understands restraint, the bun substantial enough to hold together without overwhelming. Nothing pretentious, nothing unnecessary—just honest food executed with care.

"He did this for you? For free?" The critic in me is always suspicious of motives.

Ruth snorts. "Wouldn't take a dime. Said it was payment for all the free advice his granddad gave him over this very bar."

"Hunter's grandfather was a fixture here?"

The question opens a floodgate. The white-haired man—Jim, retired from forty years in the now-closed silver mine—moves to join me at the bar. The story of Hunter Morgan and his grandfather unfolds in fragments from different voices as other patrons drift over.

Old Man Morgan, as they call him, was the town's unofficial caretaker after the mine closed. Head cook at the original Angel's Peak Hotel, he fed people who couldn't pay during the hardest times. When the hotel burned down in 2001, he kept cooking from his home, teaching his orphaned grandson everything he knew.

"That boy would follow him into the woods, learning which mushrooms were safe, which berries were sweetest," Ruth says, refilling my ale without being asked. "By twelve, he could field dress a deer faster than most grown men."

"When he got that fancy chef job down in Denver, we all figured he'd never come back," says a woman who introduces herself as the local librarian. "But luck has a way of circling around here."

"Luck had nothing to do with it," Jim interjects. "That business partner of his was a snake. We all saw it when he visited, though Hunter was too trusting to notice."

I think of the article my editor sent, the bankruptcy and scandal that followed. How different it sounds here, among people who've known Hunter his whole life.

"Lucas Reid was smart, bringing him back to run Timberline," Ruth says. "Old money recognizing real talent."

Another round of stories follows—how Hunter convinced Lucas to institute a local employment preference at The Haven, how he established a culinary internship program with the regional high school, and how he still finds time to help Ruth's nephew improve his brewing techniques.

I recognize the Hunter they describe—dedicated, generous with his knowledge, deeply connected to this place and its people. But there's something disconcerting about hearing it from others, realizing how little I know him beyond our intense physical connection and the glimpses he's chosen to show me.

The conversation shifts as a woman bursts through the door, breathless with excitement. "You'll never guess who confirmed for Mabel's fundraiser today! That food writer from Denver Monthly!"

My blood freezes in my veins.

"Another fancy critic?" Jim scoffs. "What do they know about real mountain cooking?"

"It's exposure," the woman insists. "And we need all we can get if we're going to save Mabel's place."

Ruth notices my confusion and explains. "Mabel Wilson runs the only guest house in town proper. Historic building, been in her family for generations. But it needs serious renovation to meet county codes. Town's been fundraising all summer."

"And Hunter's cooking," the newcomer adds, eyes bright. "Said he'd feed a hundred people if that's what it takes to keep Mabel going."

I check my watch, suddenly needing to be anywhere but

here, where my professional identity feels like a betrayal of these people's trust.

"Is this fundraiser open to anyone?" The question slips out before I can reconsider.

"Four o'clock at Mabel's. Corner of Pine and Aspen." Ruth studies me with shrewd eyes. "You thinking of coming?"

"Maybe." I leave enough cash to cover my meal and a generous tip. "Thank you for the history lesson. And the excellent burger."

Outside, I walk aimlessly through town, memories surfacing from my past—so different from the community solidarity I've just witnessed.

Growing up in a series of sterile apartments with a mother who worked two jobs and still couldn't afford fresh vegetables. The revelation of my first authentic restaurant meal at sixteen, paid for with weeks of babysitting money, showed me that food could be more than mere sustenance, that it could tell stories and create experiences.

My college years were spent waiting tables while studying journalism, allowing me to witness the power dynamics of fine dining from the service side. How I swore I'd be the critic who remembered what it felt like to choose between paying rent and eating well. How, somewhere along the way, that mission twisted into becoming The Executioner, known more for clever takedowns than championing worthy establishments.

When did I stop seeing the humans behind the restaurants I reviewed?

My feet carry me to the corner of Pine and Aspen. Mabel's Guest House is a Victorian painted lady in faded blues and creams, its wraparound porch sagging slightly but still graceful. A banner strung between porch columns reads "Save Mabel's Place - Community Fundraiser Today!"

Tables and chairs have been arranged across the expansive front lawn. A makeshift outdoor kitchen occupies one corner, where I spot Hunter's tall frame directing a small army of volunteers. He moves with the same controlled grace he shows in his professional kitchen, though dressed casually in jeans and a faded t-shirt bearing the logo of a local brewing festival.

I should leave. This is precisely the kind of community event that would make excellent color for my review, but I'm no longer pretending to be objective. Yet I find myself drawn forward, pulled by some need I can't quite name.

Hunter looks up as if sensing my presence. His face transforms, lighting with genuine pleasure that makes my chest ache.

"Audrey!" He crosses the lawn in long strides, wiping his hands on a towel tucked into his back pocket. "You found us."

"I heard about it in town." Not exactly a lie. "It seemed important."

"It is." He takes my hand, an easy gesture that feels alarmingly natural. "Mabel's is the heart of this town. Come on, I'll introduce you."

Before I can object, I'm being led through the gathering crowd. Hunter's hand warm around mine. He introduces me to what feels like half the town's population—the mayor, the elementary school principal, local artisans, and shopkeepers. To each, he says the same thing: "This is Audrey, a special friend of mine."

The simple designation warms me even as guilt twists beneath. What would these smiling people think if they knew I was here to evaluate them, to judge their beloved hometown chef? That my word could potentially devastate the economic lifeline Hunter has helped create?

"Hunter Morgan, are you going to hog that lovely young woman all to yourself?" The voice rings with authority despite its age.

A tiny woman with silver hair twisted into a crown of braids approaches, leaning on a carved wooden cane. Despite her small stature, she exudes a commanding presence. People step aside automatically.

"Gram." Hunter's face softens with unmistakable love. "I was just coming to find you. This is Audrey."

"Eleanor Morgan." She offers a hand that feels like soft paper over bird bones but grips with surprising strength. Eyes identical to Hunter's. She assess me with unnerving perception. "So you're what's had my grandson walking on air these past few days."

Heat rises to my cheeks. "I wouldn't say that."

"I would." Her laugh is unexpectedly rich for such a small frame. "Know how I can tell? He made his special wild blackberry compote this morning. He only does that when he's sweet on someone."

"Gram." Hunter's protest carries no real objection, a flush creeping up his neck.

"Hush, boy. Let me get acquainted with your girl." She loops her arm through mine, effectively separating me from Hunter. "Come help an old woman find a comfortable seat, and I'll tell you about the time Hunter decided to surprise me with breakfast in bed and set my kitchen curtains on fire."

Hunter groans but makes no move to stop her, returning to his cooking station with a backward glance that carries equal parts apology and affection.

Eleanor leads me to a table beneath a sprawling oak tree, regaling me with stories of Hunter's childhood exploits—his first disastrous attempts at cooking, his determination to master his grandfather's recipes, his teenage rebellion that took the form of attempting molecular gastronomy in their rustic kitchen.

"Nearly blew up the house trying to make some fancy foam," she chuckles. "His grandfather was furious. Not about the mess, mind you, but about wasting good ingredients on what he called 'cloud food.'"

I find myself laughing more than I have in years, charmed by her forthright manner and love for her grandson.

"He was always too serious," she continues, watching Hunter direct his volunteers. "Took everything to heart. Felt responsible for the whole world."

"He seems well-loved here," I observe, watching townspeople stop by his station, each receiving a moment of genuine attention despite his busy hands.

"This place is in his blood." Eleanor's gaze turns shrewd. "What about you, Audrey? What's in your blood?"

The question catches me off guard. "I'm not sure what you mean."

"Yes, you are." Her hand pats mine with surprising gentleness. "Everyone has something that drives them, defines them. Hunter has this place, these people. What do you have?"

The answer comes unbidden: "Words. Stories." I hesitate, then add, "Truth, I hope."

She nods as if I've confirmed something. "Good. He needs someone who understands truth. There's been too much deception in his life."

"You mean with his restaurant in Denver?" I ask carefully, wondering how much she knows.

Eleanor's eyes cloud with remembered anger. "That snake of a business partner—Garrett—was just the culmination. Hunter's always attracted people who want to use him." She leans closer, voice dropping. "Then his sous chef in Chicago stole his recipes and opened her own place."

She sighs, weathered hands folding in her lap. "Garrett was the worst, though. Manipulated investors behind Hunter's back, changed suppliers to cheaper products without telling him, then blamed kitchen failures on Hunter when customers complained. By the time Hunter discovered the financial deception, the restaurant was already sinking. Garrett had been siphoning money for months."

"Hunter never told me the details," I murmur, guilt slicing through me like a blade.

"He wouldn't. Too proud." Eleanor's piercing gaze returns to mine. "He trusts too easily, that boy. Sees the good in people. It's his gift and his curse."

The barb lands precisely, whether intentional or not. I look away, unable to meet those eyes, so like her grandson's; the weight of my own deception suddenly becomes unbearable.

"I should help with something," I say, rising. "It doesn't seem right just to sit while everyone works."

"Another good sign." Eleanor's smile warms her entire face. "Serving station needs hands, I suspect."

I find myself drafted into service, donning an apron and taking a position behind a long table laden with Hunter's creations. For the next two hours, I serve food to a steady stream of community members, learning names and connections, hearing more stories about Mabel's place and its importance to Angel's Peak.

The food Hunter has prepared is simpler than his Timberline offerings but no less thoughtful—dishes designed to be served outdoors, to hold their quality through the afternoon, to feed many from ingredients that remain affordable while showcasing local products.

I catch him watching me from across the lawn, a complicated expression on his face. When our eyes meet, something passes between us—recognition, connection, possibility. I feel myself falling deeper into whatever this is between us, whatever we might become to each other if circumstances were different.

For one suspended moment, I allow myself to imagine it— a life here, among these mountains and these people. Waking to Hunter's smile each morning. Becoming part of this community that rallies around its own. Trading my nomadic existence for roots, for belonging.

The fantasy is so vivid that it leaves me breathless.

The Denver food writer never materializes—probably stuck in mountain traffic, someone speculates. The fundraiser collects enough to repair Mabel's roof and bring the electrical system up to code. As twilight descends, someone produces fiddles and guitars, and impromptu dancing breaks out on the lawn.

Hunter finds me as I'm hanging up my serving apron. "Thank you for helping." His voice is low and intimate, beneath the music and laughter. "You didn't have to do that."

"I wanted to." The simple truth feels revolutionary on my tongue.

His hand finds mine, fingers interlacing. "You fit here." The words carry weight beyond their simplicity. "With these people. With me."

My throat tightens. I can't speak past the emotion lodged there.

"Stay." It's barely a whisper, more of a plea than a demand. "Not just for your week. Stay longer."

"Hunter—"

"I know it's fast. I know you have a life elsewhere." His eyes hold mine, nakedly vulnerable in a way I've never seen him. "But I think we could build something real here. Together."

Words fail me entirely. Instead, I rise on tiptoe and kiss him, aware of Eleanor watching from across the lawn, of townspeople noticing and smiling, of how public this declaration feels.

For once, I don't care who sees. Don't care about professional boundaries or my carefully crafted persona. In this moment, I'm just a woman kissing a man she's falling in love with, surrounded by a community that already feels partly mine.

Later, much later, I return to my room at The Haven. The night air carries the scent of pine and woodsmoke. The mountains are black silhouettes against a star-strewn sky. Hunter offered to walk me back, but I needed time alone, and space to think.

My laptop sits where I left it this morning, both drafts of my review still open and unsent. I read through them again—the expected takedown and the honest appreciation, the critic's voice and the woman's heart.

With sudden clarity, I know which is true. Know which I can live with publishing.

I make a few final edits, attach Hunter's grandfather's trout recipe photos, and press send on one of the drafts. Then I close my laptop, unexpectedly at peace with my decision.

My phone rings almost immediately. My editor's name flashes on the screen.

I answer, heart suddenly racing.

"Audrey." Her voice carries confusion and something like concern. "This isn't what I expected from you. Are you sure about this?"

Angel's Peak

Chapter 10

Brewing Storm

THE STORM ARRIVES WITH A VENGEANCE NO ONE predicted.

I wake to darkness so complete I think it must still be night until I check my phone. 8:17 AM. The screen's glow illuminates swirling white beyond my window—snow falling with such intensity that the mountains have vanished completely, erased by a wall of white.

A text from Hunter awaits: *"Check outside your door."*

I wrap myself in the plush robe hanging in the bathroom and open my suite door to find a thermos, a basket of still-warm pastries, and a handwritten note: *"Storm knocked out power. Generator running for essentials only. Stay warm. Will check on you later. -H"*

The gesture warms me more than the coffee, which turns out to be perfect, strong and laced with cinnamon and something else I can't quite identify. The pastries are Hunter's creation, I'm certain—delicate layers that shatter beautifully, filled with local preserves.

My editor hasn't called again since our brief, confused conversation last night. After her initial surprise at my glowing review of Timberline, she recovered quickly, shifting to practicalities—timeline, photos, headline options. I ended the call before she could ask too many questions about my uncharacteristic praise.

Now, watching the blizzard transform the landscape into something alien and dangerous, I wonder if this storm is some cosmic reflection of my internal turbulence.

The power flickers, then stabilizes at half-strength. Emergency lighting casts an amber glow through the hallways as I venture out, dressed in my warmest clothes. Other guests huddle in the main lobby where staff distribute blankets and hot beverages. The massive stone fireplace roars with fresh-cut logs, becoming the heart of the improvised refugee camp.

"Haven't seen a storm like this in September for twenty years." A maintenance worker feeds another log into the flames. "Three feet already and more coming. Roads are closed in both directions."

"What about the town? Are they okay?" I'm surprised by how quickly my concern turns to the people I met yesterday—Ruth at The Pickaxe, Mabel with her historic guest house, Eleanor with her perceptive eyes.

"Angel's Peak folk know how to handle weather." The man nods with certainty. "Been doing it for generations. It's you flatlanders we worry about."

A commotion at the main entrance draws attention. Hunter stamps in, snow coating his shoulders and hair, carrying crates of supplies. Several kitchen staff follow, similarly burdened. His eyes find mine across the crowded room, a brief connection before duty calls him back to work.

For the next few hours, I watch him move through the lodge—checking on elderly guests, organizing his kitchen staff to provide hot food despite limited power, coordinating with maintenance on generator priorities. His leadership style remains the same as in his kitchen—calm, decisive, focused on others' needs before his own.

By late afternoon, the storm shows no signs of abating. The world outside has disappeared entirely, the windows nothing but rectangles of impenetrable white. I've migrated to a corner armchair with a borrowed paperback, trying to lose myself in fiction rather than dwell on the reality of my situation.

"You look comfortable." Hunter appears beside me, the first chance he's had to approach all day. Despite hours of crisis management, he seems energized rather than exhausted. "How are you holding up?"

"Better than most." I nod toward a family with restless children, parents looking increasingly frazzled. "Though I'm running out of distractions."

"I might have a solution for that." He glances at his watch. "Kitchen's under control for the next hour. Want to see something?"

Curiosity piqued, I follow him through service corridors and up a narrow staircase I didn't know existed. We emerge into a small observatory perched at the highest point of the lodge. Floor-to-ceiling windows on three sides would normally showcase a panoramic view of the mountains. Today, they display nothing but churning snow and the occasional flash of ice crystals caught in the exterior lights.

"It's beautiful, in its way." I approach the glass, feeling the cold radiating from the surface. "Terrifying, but beautiful."

"Nature's reminder that we're not in charge." Hunter stands close enough that I feel his warmth. "No matter how much we think we've tamed this place."

The room holds several telescopes and star charts, apparently used for guest activities on clear nights. A small seating area occupies one corner, and Hunter guides me there, producing a flask from inside his jacket.

"Emergency supplies." He pours amber liquid into two tumblers. "My grandfather's whiskey. He distilled it himself."

The spirit burns pleasantly as it goes down, warming me from the inside with notes of honey, oak, and something uniquely mountain—perhaps the spring water used in its creation.

"You've been amazing today." I gesture vaguely toward the lodge below. "Taking care of everyone."

He shrugs, uncomfortable with the praise. "It's what needs doing."

"It's more than that." I turn to face him fully. "You care. Genuinely care about all of them. It's not just professional responsibility."

"These mountains raised me." He stares into his glass. "The people here looked after me and Gram after my parents died. When my grandfather passed three years ago, they became my family." He takes another sip, eyes reflecting the whiskey's color. "I owe them everything."

"Is that why you came back? After Denver?"

Pain flickers across his features. "Partly. Also, because I had nowhere else to go." His admission carries raw honesty. "The restaurant's failure nearly broke me. Not financially—though that was bad enough—but here." He taps his chest. "I started to believe what they were saying about me."

"What, who was saying?"

"Critics. Former employees who jumped ship. Industry people who love watching a rising star crash and burn." Bitterness edges his voice for the first time since I've known him. "That I was overrated. A flash in the pan. That I'd reached beyond my abilities."

I think of my cutting reviews and how I never considered their impact beyond circulation numbers and professional reputation. How many chefs had I wounded with clever turns of phrase meant more to entertain readers than provide constructive criticism?

"Lucas gave me a lifeline when no one else would." Hunter continues, unaware of my internal reckoning. "He remembered me from culinary school—he was a guest lecturer, inherited wealth with a passion for food. When he took over this property from his grandfather and developed The Haven into what it is now, he offered me Timberline."

"Sounds like a good friend."

"Cousin, actually, and he is." Hunter's use of past tense catches my attention. "Until recently."

"What changed?"

"Money. Investors." He sighs, refilling our glasses. "The Haven isn't performing as expected. Timberline does well, but the rooms aren't booking at the projected rates. The investors are pressuring him."

"And he's pressuring you."

His laugh holds no humor. "Last week, he suggested we 'pivot the concept.' Make Timberline more accessible. Add burger night and pasta specials." His hand tightens around his glass. "Everything my grandfather taught me about honoring ingredients, about cooking with integrity—Lucas wants to sacrifice it for profit margins."

"What will you do?" The question emerges barely above a whisper.

"Fight." Determination hardens his features. "This kitchen is my second chance. I won't compromise what makes it special." His eyes find mine, vulnerability beneath the resolve. "But I'm afraid of failing. Of letting down the people who believed in me when no one else would."

The confession hangs between us, weighted with trust I haven't earned. I should tell him who I am and what I've done, but the words stick in my throat, selfish fear winning out over honesty.

"You won't fail." Instead, I reach for him, hand resting against his cheek.

"You sound certain." He turns his face into my palm, lips brushing my skin.

"I am." At least in this, I can be honest. My review will ensure it.

"Remember what you told me? In the cabin?" His demeanor shifts subtly, eyes darkening as he catches my wrist. "About liking when I take charge." His thumb traces circles against my pulse point. "Did you mean it?"

"Yes." Heat floods my body at the memory.

"Would you let me do that now?"

His voice is low. Rough velvet. A question—and a promise. "Really take control?"

My breath catches. The air thickens between us, charged with the weight of what he's asking. It's not just about tonight. It's about everything. About trust. About surrender. About what I want—maybe even what I need.

I meet his eyes. "What did you have in mind?" Anticipation coils low in my belly.

"Trust me?" He doesn't wait for an answer. Just reaches into his back pocket and pulls out a black silk handkerchief— folded and worn, soft with use.

A pulse of heat surges through me.

He moves behind me without a word, the silk sliding across my cheek, my temple. Then over my eyes. Darkness closes in, silencing everything but the drumbeat of my heart and the sound of his breath—steady, sure, closer than I thought.

"Stand." The command comes quietly but firmly.

My legs wobble slightly as I rise. His hands find my waist, large and warm, grounding me.

"I'm going to touch you now." His voice in my ear sends

shivers down my spine. "You can say stop at any time. Understand?"

"Yes."

He takes my hand and leads me. Each step unfamiliar. I brush against something—a table, maybe—a chair leg. Then cool air wraps around me, and I realize we're near the window.

"Hands above your head."

I lift them. Fingers searching.

He binds my wrists together with something soft and smooth —his scarf, I think—then fastens it to something overhead. My arms stretch. My back arches. I'm exposed. Suspended. Vulnerable in a way that makes my thighs clench and my breath catch.

Without sight, I'm entirely in his control, surrendering to sensation in a way I've never experienced. The cold of the window seeps through my clothes, a shocking contrast to the heat building within me.

"Hands above your head." Another quiet command.

I comply, feeling something soft—his scarf, I realize— being wound around my wrists, binding them together and then to something above me. The position leaves me open, vulnerable, entirely at his mercy.

"Still okay?" he checks, hands hovering at my sides.

"More than okay." My voice emerges breathless with anticipation.

His touch, when it comes, is both tender and commanding. His fingertips skim my shoulders. My chest. My sides. Not grabbing. Not rushing. Mapping me.

He takes his time undressing me, each newly exposed patch of skin receiving focused attention from his hands and his mouth. The contrast of cold air and his warm touch creates a symphony of sensations that makes me gasp.

The cool air teases my nipples instantly, making them pebble.

I gasp.

He hums behind me, pleased.

"You're beautiful like this." His voice roughens with desire. "Surrendering control. Trusting me to give you what you need."

Then his mouth closes over one.

My knees buckle.

He suckles and licks, then flicks just hard enough to make me cry out. His hands knead my breasts as he feasts on them like he's starving. I writhe, trapped and helpless, the blindfold sharpening every touch to a razor's edge.

My jeans are next. He unbuttons them, slides them down slowly, letting the denim drag along my thighs, my calves. I'm wet. Soaked. And he hasn't even touched me there yet.

He doesn't rush. Doesn't speak. Just peels my panties down with aching deliberation.

Then his fingers are on me.

Two slide between my thighs, stroking through the slick heat. A soft curse escapes him—low and reverent.

"You're dripping," he growls, voice thick with need. "You like being blindfolded and bound."

A whimper slips from my lips.

He teases me—fingers brushing my clit, then retreating. Circling my entrance, then pulling away. I jerk my hips, desperate for more. He denies me. Again. Again.

"Please," I gasp, straining against the scarf above me. "Hunter—please—"

A sharp slap lands on my inner thigh. Not hard enough to hurt. Just enough to claim.

"You don't get to beg. Not yet."

Another stroke, firmer now. He slips a finger inside me, slow and deep. My head tips back. A moan escapes me.

Then another finger joins the first. He fucks me with them

—steady, controlled. Thumb brushing my clit in perfect rhythm until I'm panting.

"Close?" His voice is pure sin. "You want to come?"

"Yes," I cry. "Yes, please—"

He pulls away.

I sob.

He laughs—low, dark, pleased.

"You'll wait. You'll come when I say. Not a second before."

Then his mouth is on me.

Hot. Wet. Devastating.

He licks through my folds, tongue pressing deep before circling up to my clit. His hands grip my thighs, holding me wide, holding me open as he devours me.

No teasing now. Just ruthless focus.

I scream his name. I thrash. I can't see, can't fight, can't hide. He doesn't stop. Not when I shudder. Not when my legs tremble. Not even when I plead with broken breath.

"Please—Hunter—I can't—"

"Not yet."

He slides his fingers back inside me, mouth still latched onto my clit, working me with a precision that borders on cruel.

I break.

Everything inside me unravels. I fall apart in waves—screaming, sobbing, shaking so hard the scarf creaks above me.

And still—he doesn't stop. Not until I'm completely wrecked.

Only then does he release me.

He unbinds my wrists gently, catches me when I collapse. I'm weightless. Boneless. Floating somewhere between heaven and hell and unable to tell the difference.

He lifts me, carries me like something precious, and lays me on the couch, wrapping me in a blanket pulled from the back.

I curl into his chest, blindfold still on, senses raw and open.

"That was..." My voice cracks. I don't even try to finish.

His arms close around me, and he kisses the top of my head.

"You were perfect."

His lips graze my temple as I lay limp in his arms, cocooned in the afterglow and the faintest tremors of release still twitching in my thighs.

But he's not finished. Not even close.

I feel it—the tension in his muscles, the throb of him hard against my hip, restrained too long. His breath is shallow, his control stretched taut.

I slide my hand down his stomach, fingers brushing the waistband of his jeans. He catches my wrist.

"No." His voice is hoarse. Dangerous. "You're not the one taking care of me tonight."

My breath hitches. The blindfold is still in place. I can't see him—but I feel the shift. The moment his restraint snaps and he lets go.

He stands, stripping silently. I hear the metallic rasp of his belt, the soft thud of boots hitting the floor, and then—

"On your knees."

I scramble to obey, the wool blanket falling away. The floor is cold beneath me, but it doesn't matter. I kneel where he left me: naked, blindfolded, wrists still warm from the scarf.

A hand fists gently in my hair, guiding me forward. His cock brushes my lips—hot, heavy, demanding.

"Open," he murmurs. "Suck my cock. Show me how eagerly you serve."

I open for him willingly, tongue flicking the tip before taking him deep. His fingers tighten in my hair as a groan tears from his throat.

"Fuck..."

He holds still for a beat, letting me adjust, then begins to thrust—not gently. Not slowly. He takes my mouth like he owns it, like he owns me. Each stroke deliberate, hips snapping with the same controlled force he used on my body before.

"Look at you," he growls, breath ragged. "So fucking beautiful like this. On your knees. Mine."

Tears prick beneath the blindfold as I struggle to breathe through the intensity of it—of him—but I don't want it to stop.

He withdraws suddenly, dragging me to my feet. Spinning me.

"Hands on the couch. Ass up."

I brace myself, heart thundering. My legs barely hold me, but I obey.

Then he enters me from behind in one powerful thrust.

I cry out—half-shock, half ecstasy. He's thick and deep and relentless, driving into me with punishing force, each thrust a possession, a claim. One hand fists in my hair, pulling my head back, the other spans my hip, holding me exactly where he wants me.

"You feel this?" he grits. "This is what I've been holding back." He slaps my ass—sharp, delicious. My body jolts. My moan echoes off the walls. He fucks me harder.

Raw. Primal. Unleashed.

My arms buckle beneath me. I'm nothing but sensation now—blinded, bound, wrecked and remade by every stroke.

My body pulses with another orgasm—sharp and sudden, almost painful in its intensity.

I scream his name.

He follows with a low, guttural growl, his body driving deep one last time as he spills inside me, holding me flush to him as we both fall apart.

When it's over, he doesn't let go. He wraps around me

from behind, breath warm against my neck, and slowly—gently—slides the blindfold free.

His voice, when he finally speaks again, is a whisper.

"You gave me everything tonight."

"That was amazing." In his arms, ruined and cherished all at once, I know it's true.

"I know." He presses a kiss to my temple. "For me, too."

We remain there as the storm rages outside, the violence of nature a counterpoint to the peace I've found in his arms. Eventually, duty calls him back downstairs—guests to check on, staff to coordinate, and a thousand small crises demanding attention.

"Stay here as long as you like." He kisses me deeply before leaving. "It's our secret place now."

I must drift off eventually, lulled by the whiskey and emotional exhaustion. When I wake, the storm has subsided to gentle snowfall, and moonlight occasionally breaks through clouds to illuminate the transformed landscape. A blanket has been draped over me—Hunter must have returned while I slept.

He sits at a small desk in the corner, the lamp's glow creating a pool of light around him. His focus is absolute as he sketches in a worn notebook, unaware I'm watching.

"What are you working on?" My voice, thick with sleep, startles him.

"Sorry, didn't mean to wake you." He turns the notebook toward me. "Ideas for Timberline. Menu expansions, new techniques for preserving seasonal ingredients."

I examine his work—detailed sketches of plating designs, notes on flavor combinations, and calculations for food costs. The pages reveal the mind of a chef who is constantly evolving and seeking improvement.

"Even with everything happening, you're still planning for the future." Admiration colors my voice.

"Especially with everything happening." Determination sets his jaw. "This place will succeed. I'll make it work, whatever it takes."

Looking at his plans and hopes sketched carefully, I understand with painful clarity what my review means. It's not just about a restaurant or a chef's ego. It's about this man's redemption, his community's economic lifeline, his family's legacy.

I'm grateful now for my decision and for the truth I chose to tell in my final draft.

We return to my suite as false dawn breaks over the snow-covered mountains. The power has stabilized enough for heat and basic lighting. Hunter needs to check on the restaurant and assess any damage from the storm.

"I'll come find you later." He kisses me at my door, lingering as if reluctant to leave. "Once I know everything's secure."

After he's gone, I check my phone, and cellphone reception has returned with the storm's passing. Multiple notifications await, most urgently, an email from my editor.

My stomach drops as I read the message: *"Final version attached. Publishing tomorrow online, print next week. Last chance for changes."*

The attachment contains my review—the honest, glowing assessment of Timberline's brilliance—with minor edits for length and house style. Relief floods through me. She accepted my perspective and didn't try to push me back toward my usual critical voice.

As I scan the document, confirming all is as it should be, a text arrives with a distinctive ping.

My editor again: *"Final version attached. Publishing tomorrow online, print next week. Last chance for changes."*

I frown, confused by the duplicate message, until I open the attachment.

Horror washes through me in an icy wave.

This isn't my review. Not the one I submitted.

This is the other draft—the cutting, clever takedown that questions Timberline's originality and dismisses Hunter's cuisine as derivative mountain fare elevated by pretentious technique. The Executioner's voice is sharp and merciless, dismantling everything Hunter has built with surgical precision.

My fingers tremble as I dial my editor's number, desperation clawing at my throat. The call goes straight to voicemail.

I try again.

Same result.

Frantically, I type a response: "WRONG VERSION. Do NOT publish this. Call me IMMEDIATELY."

The message shows as delivered but not read. I call the magazine's main line, but it's Saturday—no one will be in the office.

Outside my window, the sun breaks through the clouds, illuminating a world transformed by the storm—beautiful, pristine, and utterly changed. Just like my life was beginning to be, before this catastrophic error.

My phone pings again.

"Final version attached. Publishing tomorrow online, print next week. Last chance for changes."

Angel's Peak

CHAPTER 11

TRUTH AND CONSEQUENCES

PANIC CLAWS AT MY THROAT AS I STARE AT MY phone screen, desperately willing my editor to respond. Three texts, five calls—all unanswered. The wrong version of my review sits in her inbox, poised to destroy everything I've come to care about. Everything Hunter has built.

I have until tomorrow—less than twenty-four hours to fix this catastrophic error.

But even if I succeed, a deeper truth remains: Hunter doesn't know who I am or what I came here to do. Every moment I've spent with him has been built on a foundation of deception, regardless of how real my feelings have become.

I dress quickly—dark jeans, burgundy sweater, boots appropriate for the snow-covered ground. My reflection shows a woman I barely recognize, eyes haunted by the weight of a necessary confession.

The Haven has sprung back to life after the storm. Staff clear paths through knee-deep snow, and guests venture outside to marvel at the transformed landscape. The sense of shared crisis has created a strange camaraderie among strangers.

I barely notice any of it, my mind fixed on a single purpose as I make my way to Timberline. The restaurant is located in its own wing of the lodge, accessible both from within and via a separate entrance for non-hotel guests. I choose the external path, needing these few minutes in the biting cold to clear my head and rehearse what I'll say.

I need to tell you something. I haven't been honest about who I am. I'm the food critic for Palette Magazine. I came here to review Timberline, but I never expected to meet you, to feel this connection...

No matter how I phrase it, the truth sounds hollow and self-serving.

The restaurant's entrance is partially blocked by drifted snow, but the door yields when I push. Inside, controlled chaos reigns. Staff hurry between stations, checking inventory and assessing storm damage. A ceiling leak has been contained with the strategic placement of pots and buckets. The massive windows, typically showcasing mountain views, are still partially obscured by ice and snow.

Hunter stands at the center, sleeves rolled to his elbows, issuing instructions with calm authority despite the dark circles under his eyes suggesting he hasn't slept. He hasn't noticed me yet, giving me a moment to observe him in his element—focused, decisive, and completely in command of his domain despite the crisis.

Courage nearly fails me. How can I shatter this man's world? Yet how can I not tell him before he discovers the truth from someone else?

He looks up, eyes finding mine across the room. His expression softens instantly, worry lines easing as he changes course to approach me.

"Hey." His voice drops for my ears alone as he reaches me. "I was going to come find you once we got this under control."

"I need to see you." My voice sounds strained. "To talk to you about something important."

Concern shadows his features. "Everything okay?"

"Not exactly. I need to—"

"Hunter!" A server hurries over with a clipboard. "The seafood delivery can't get through. Rockslide on the pass."

Hunter's focus shifts, his professional responsibilities taking priority over our conversation. "Call Marie at High Country Farms. See if she can increase our meat order. And check with Javier about additional vegetable options." He turns back to me. "Sorry. Give me just a few minutes?"

Those few minutes stretch to thirty as one crisis after another demands his attention. I hover at the edges of the activity, watching Hunter navigate each challenge with the same grace he brings to creating his dishes.

A distinguished dark-haired man in an impeccably tailored suit enters, surveying the situation with a critical eye. Lucas Reid, I presume. His presence changes the energy in the room immediately—staff stand straighter, voices lower, movement becomes more purposeful.

"Morgan." His voice carries both authority and concern. "How do things look?"

Hunter straightens, meeting his gaze directly. "Minimal structural damage. One leak contained. We've lost the seafood delivery due to road conditions, but we're adapting the menu. We can open for dinner service tonight with a limited selection."

"Cancellations?" Lucas asks.

"Three so far. We're calling to confirm the remaining reservations."

Lucas nods, seemingly satisfied. His gaze sweeps the room, landing on me with sudden interest. "And who is this?"

Hunter's expression shifts subtly—protective, possessive. "Audrey Tristan. A... friend."

Lucas approaches, offering a manicured hand. "Lucas Reid. A pleasure, Ms. Tristan. Are you enjoying your stay at The Haven?"

"Very much," I respond, shaking his hand. "You've created something special here."

"Hunter is responsible for Haven's success." His tone suggests this is both a compliment and an expectation. He turns back to Hunter. "We need to discuss the financial implications of yesterday's closure. My office, thirty minutes."

"I'll be there." Hunter's jaw tightens almost imperceptibly.

As Lucas departs, Hunter rubs the back of his neck, tension radiating from his posture. "Sorry about this. Not exactly how I planned to spend time with you today."

"I understand." I step closer, lowering my voice. "Hunter, I really need to tell you something."

"Chef!" His sous chef appears, panic evident. "The walk-in's temperature is fluctuating. We might lose everything if the compressor's damaged."

Hunter curses under his breath. "I need to handle this." Regret fills his eyes. "Can it wait? I promise I'll make time for us later."

The coward in me seizes the reprieve. "I can help if you need extra hands."

Relief washes over his features. "That would be amazing. We're short-staffed with people unable to make it in."

Before I can reconsider, I'm being handed an apron, integrated into Timberline's emergency response. For the next two hours, I work alongside Hunter and his team, inventorying the surviving ingredients, helping to revise the menu based on available products, and preparing vegetables for dinner service.

The work is physical and immediate, requiring full concentration. Hunter moves around the kitchen, occasionally passing behind me with a hand at the small of my back, our bodies unconsciously finding synchronicity in the shared space.

"You're good at this," he comments, watching me julienne carrots with surprising precision. "Are you sure you haven't worked in a kitchen before?"

"I picked up a few things over the years." It's not technically a lie, but my stomach twists nonetheless.

We're alone in the walk-in refrigerator when the mounting tension between us finally breaks. Hunter has been checking the repaired cooling system to ensure the temperature remains stable, thereby preserving his precious ingredients. I'm behind him, cataloging the cheese selection that survived the power fluctuations.

"I think we're back to normal," he says, making a note on his clipboard. "Crisis averted."

"Good." I reach past him for a wheel of aged cheddar, my body brushing against his.

The simple contact ignites something primal. His clipboard clatters to the floor as he turns, backing me against the stainless steel shelving. One hand braces beside my head, and the other is already sliding under the hem of my sweater. His mouth finds mine with devastating precision, and his hands grip my hips to pull me flush against him.

The refrigerator's cold air clings to my skin, but I don't feel it. Not with the heat radiating off him, not with his hands gripping my waist like he's seconds from unraveling.

"We shouldn't," I whisper against his mouth, my breath already gone. "Your staff—"

His lips trail down my jaw. "Don't care." His voice is a low rasp against my neck. "Been watching you in my kitchen all day. Do you have any idea what that does to me?"

His hand slides beneath my sweater, palm flat against my stomach, fingers splayed possessively. I arch into his touch, all thoughts of confession temporarily burned away by more immediate need.

His fingers fumble at the button of my jeans. I clutch at his shirt, the fabric in my fists grounding me as he yanks the zipper down and pushes my jeans over my hips. Cold air rushes in—then vanishes as his hand slides between my thighs, sure and possessive.

"You're burning up," he murmurs, voice shaking now. "Fuck, Audrey."

My hands dive beneath his chef's coat, searching for skin and the taut muscles I remember. I find them—solid and hot—and press my palms against his stomach, his chest, needing all of him at once.

"Five minutes," he murmurs, lifting me onto a cleared shelf. "Give me five minutes."

He shoves his pants down just enough and lifts me in one smooth motion. I wrap my legs around him, the shelving cold and sharp against my spine, his hands hard beneath my thighs.

He pushes inside me in one deep stroke, and I gasp—head falling back against the metal, pleasure spiking through my entire body.

"God," he breathes. "I forgot..."

He doesn't finish. Just moves. Thrusting into me with a desperate rhythm, hands everywhere—gripping my hips, sliding under my sweater to find skin, cupping my breast through my bra as his mouth claims mine again.

I hold on—arms wrapped around his neck, breath caught in my throat—each grind of his hips sending sparks through my core.

There's no finesse. No patience. Just need compacted into a frantic rhythm of soft moans, quick gasps, and bodies colliding in the cold.

"I'm close," I whisper against his ear, nails digging into his back.

"Me too," he groans, thrusting harder. "Don't stop—just stay with me—"

And I do.

I break first, clenching around him as pleasure rips through me, sharp and fast. He follows seconds later, hips jerking once, twice more as he spills inside me, breath caught in his throat.

We stay like that, frozen in the aftermath—his forehead resting against mine, breath coming in white puffs between us.

Neither of us speaks.

There's only the sound of our breathing, the fridge's hum, and my heartbeat pounding inside my chest.

Then, quietly, like he's not sure he should say it at all—

"I'm falling in love with you."

The words land like an avalanche.

My heart simultaneously soars and plummets. "Hunter—" I swallow hard, heart tripping.

"I know." He tucks a strand of hair behind my ear with surprising tenderness, given our hasty coupling. "I know you have a life elsewhere, but I've never felt this connected to anyone."

He helps me down from the shelf, both of us adjusting our clothing with slightly shaky hands.

"Stay." His eyes hold mine, vulnerability naked in their depths. "Not just for this week. Stay longer. Give us a real chance."

The moment to confess is now before his hopes build any further. Before more damage is done.

"There's something you need to know about me." I force the words past the tightness in my throat.

"Whatever it is, it doesn't matter." He takes my hands in his. "The past is—"

The walk-in door swings open, his sous chef's voice

cutting through our bubble. "Chef, Lucas is looking for you. Says it's urgent."

Hunter sighs, squeezing my hands once before releasing them. "We'll finish this conversation later, I promise."

As we emerge from the refrigerator, several staff members exchange knowing glances. Our absence—and its nature—hasn't gone unnoticed. Under different circumstances, I might be embarrassed. Now, I'm too preoccupied with the confession hanging unspoken between us.

Hunter's phone buzzes in his pocket as we cross the kitchen. Then again. And again. He frowns, pulling it out to check the screen.

"What the hell?" Confusion crosses his features as he scrolls through notifications. "My phone's blowing up with messages."

My blood turns to ice. It can't be. Not already.

He stops walking abruptly, staring at his screen with growing amazement. "It's... it's a review. Of Timberline." His voice rises with excitement. "In Palette Magazine. They've published online ahead of print."

The floor seems to tilt beneath my feet.

"It's... incredible." Wonder fills his voice as he continues reading. "Listen to this: 'Chef Morgan's connection to place transcends mere farm-to-table trendiness, creating instead a profound dialogue between landscape and plate that only a native son could achieve.'"

Relief floods through me so intensely that I have to grasp the edge of a prep table for support. They published the right version—my honest assessment, not the cutting takedown that would have destroyed him.

Hunter continues reading aloud, and his staff gathers around him as he shares passages from my review. I hear my own words—about his innovative techniques, respect for ingredients, and ability to translate mountain terroir into unforgettable dining experiences. With each sentence, his face brightens, years of doubt and struggle visibly lifting from his shoulders.

"This changes everything." He looks up, eyes shining. "A feature review in Palette will bring in the clients Lucas has been wanting."

His sous chef claps him on the shoulder. "Couldn't happen to a more deserving chef."

The kitchen erupts in celebration. Someone produces a bottle of champagne reserved for special occasions. Glasses are distributed, and a toast is proposed to Hunter's success.

I accept a glass mechanically, my heart pounding as I wait for the other shoe to drop, for Hunter to see the byline, for him to make the connection.

"Wait, there are pictures." He returns to his phone, scrolling further. "A trout dish—my grandfather's recipe?"

His brow furrows slightly. "How did they—" He stops mid-sentence, eyes lifting to find mine across the room.

Recognition dawns slowly, then all at once. His expression shifts from confusion to understanding, and then betrayal in the space of a heartbeat. The champagne glass in his hand lowers.

"Audrey Tristan." He says my name differently now, testing it with new awareness. "'You're *The Executioner*?"

The kitchen falls silent; staff sense the sudden shift but do not understand its cause.

Hunter moves toward me, each step measured and deliberate. When he reaches me, his voice is low and controlled but edged with pain that cuts deeper than anger ever could.

"You lied to me."

Angel's Peak

CHAPTER 12

FALLOUT

HUNTER'S WORDS HANG BETWEEN US, SLICING through the warmth that filled the kitchen moments ago. His eyes—those that looked at me with desire, tenderness, and what I began to believe was love—have gone cold. The transformation is so complete that it steals my breath.

"Hunter, I can explain—" My voice sounds foreign to my ears, small and desperate.

"Explain what?" The muscle in his jaw jumps as he clenches his teeth. His hands—those strong, capable hands that explored every inch of my body just minutes ago—curl into fists at his sides. "Explain how you came here to dissect my restaurant. How you slept with me while taking mental notes for your review?"

The accusation burns like acid. "That's not what happened."

"No?" He grabs his phone, scrolls to the article that's just published, and reads it aloud. "'Chef Morgan's delicate handling of the native mountain trout showcases his reverence for local ingredients, the pine-smoked flavor evoking memories of wilderness campfires.' Tell me, Audrey—or should I call you by your byline?—was that before or after I took you against the refrigerator door?"

My cheeks flame with shame. Not because the words aren't true—they are, every syllable written from my heart—but because the timing makes them seem calculating, crafted from our intimacy rather than my honest assessment.

"I was *trying* to tell you." The protest sounds hollow even to me.

"When?" Hunter slams his phone down on the steel prep table. The clatter makes me flinch. "After publication? After you left town? Or were you planning to ghost me completely, disappear back to your city life with your secret intact?"

"Today. I came here to tell you *today*. I've been trying to tell you all day."

A harsh laugh escapes him. "Convenient timing."

The kitchen feels suddenly airless, the walls closing in around us. Staff members hover at the periphery, pretending not to watch the implosion of whatever Hunter and I were building.

"The review is good." I reach for him, but he steps back as if my touch might burn. "I fought my editor to publish it this way. She wanted something more sensational, more..."

"More like what The Executioner usually writes?" His voice drops dangerously low. "Is that supposed to make me feel special? Grateful?"

"I'm not asking for gratitude. I'm asking for understanding." Tears press hot behind my eyes, but I refuse to let them fall. "What happened between us—that wasn't research or manipulation. It was real."

"Was it?" Hunter rakes a hand through his hair, leaving it standing on end. "How would I know? Everything about you has been a lie."

"Not everything." I step forward, desperation making me brave. "Not how I feel about you. Not what happened in the greenhouse, or the cabin, or in your kitchen. Not how you've made me feel more alive in a week than I've felt in years."

Something flickers in his eyes for a heartbeat—a momentary softening, a willingness to listen. Then the kitchen door swings open, and Lucas Reid strides in, oblivious to the emotional carnage he's walking into.

"Hunter! Have you seen the review?" Lucas's face glows with triumph, tablet clutched in his hand. "The Executioner—THE Executioner—just called Timberline 'the most exciting culinary destination in the mountain region.' Reservations are already pouring in."

Hunter's gaze slides from Lucas to me, the betrayal fresh and raw in his expression.

"Lucas," Hunter's voice is controlled and professional. "Meet Audrey Tristan, food critic and The Executioner herself."

Lucas blinks, looking between us as realization dawns. "You're—"

"She was just leaving." Hunter turns his back on me, focusing on the *mise en place* arranged on the counter.

"Hunter—" I reach for him again.

"Don't." The word is soft but final. "Please respect me enough to leave now."

Lucas, finally sensing the tension, clears his throat. "I'll give you two a moment. Hunter, when you're done, I want to discuss some ideas for capitalizing on this publicity."

The door swings shut behind him, leaving us in a silence that aches.

"I never meant to hurt you." My voice breaks over the words.

Hunter doesn't look up from the vegetables he's viciously chopping. "Ask yourself something, Audrey. Would your review have been different if you hadn't fallen into bed with me?"

The question lands like a blow. Because the honest answer —the one that would hurt him more—is yes. Not because my professional assessment of his food would have changed but because I wouldn't have seen the heart behind it. I wouldn't have foraged with him in the mountains, wouldn't have watched him cook for the town fundraiser with such genuine care, and wouldn't have understood how his food told the story of this place and these people.

"That's what I thought." He reads my silence as confirmation. "Please go."

There's nothing left to say. My feet carry me through the dining room, where Lucas stands with his tablet, already making calls about expanded hours. The hostess who seated me on my first visit offers a confused smile. Outside, the mountain air that had seemed so crisp and promising now feels thin and insufficient to fill my lungs.

I walk blindly, letting my feet guide me while my mind replays every moment with Hunter, now tainted by this ending. I find myself at Maggie's Diner, the bell announcing my entrance just as it did that first day.

The red vinyl booth squeaks as I slide into it. A waitress approaches with coffee without my asking.

"You look like you need this, honey." She sets the mug down with a motherly pat on my hand.

The simple kindness undoes me. A tear escapes, then another, until I'm pressing a paper napkin to my eyes.

"Man trouble?" Darlene doesn't wait for an answer. "Best cure is Maggie's apple pie. On the house."

The pie arrives golden and fragrant, but I can't bring myself to taste it. My phone buzzes with a text from my editor.

Readers love the review. Surprising angle from you. Softer. Have you lost your edge?

The words blur through my tears. Have I lost my edge? Or found something I never knew I was missing?

Two stools down at the counter, an elderly woman with a cloud of white hair watches me over her coffee cup. "You're her, aren't you? The writer who wrote about Hunter's place."

I nod, bracing for either gratitude or hostility. The town's loyalty to Hunter runs deep, as does the gossip.

"My grandson works as a dishwasher there." She sips her coffee. "Says the review's already bringing in calls. Might need to hire more help."

"That's... good." My voice is hollow.

"You the reason Hunter looked like he'd been gut-punched. My nephew's words?"

I look up, startled by her directness. "You know Hunter?"

"Honey, everyone knows everyone in Angel's Peak. And everyone knows something's been happening between you two." She slides over to the booth across from me. "I'm Edith. Post office forty-two years."

"Audrey." I extend my hand automatically.

"I know who you are." She doesn't elaborate. "So, what happened? You wrote a good review. Boy should be over the moon."

"I didn't tell him who I was." The confession comes easier with this stranger. "I was trying, before the review came out, but he found out afterward."

Edith clicks her tongue. "Pride. Men have too much of it. Especially that one."

"He has every right to be angry."

"Sure he does. Question is, what are you going to do about it?"

I stare at her. "Do? There's nothing to do. He made it clear he wants me gone."

"And you always do what men tell you?" Edith arches an

eyebrow. "Doesn't sound like the woman who wrote that review."

My phone buzzes again. More texts, emails, and notifications as the review circulates. The online version already has hundreds of comments. My editor wants to discuss a feature on mountain cuisine. My assistant asks about follow-up restaurants to visit.

The life I built is calling me back, but it suddenly seems hollow. Empty words about food that never filled the gnawing vacancy inside me. Not the way Angel's Peak has. Not the way Hunter did.

"I should pack." I leave cash on the table despite Darlene's offer of free pie. "My flight's tomorrow."

Back at The Haven, I mechanically fold clothes into my suitcase. Each item reminds me of a moment with Hunter—the sweater I wore foraging, the dress from our first dinner, the shirt he peeled off me in the greenhouse. I should burn them all, artifacts of a week that changed everything and ultimately led nowhere.

A knock at the door interrupts my melancholy. Probably housekeeping. I open it to find Hunter's grandmother, Eleanor, her weathered face grave.

"Mrs. Morgan." I step back, surprised.

"You're packing." She nods at the open suitcase. "Running away."

"Your grandson made it clear I'm not welcome here anymore."

"My grandson is a stubborn fool." She enters uninvited, surveying the room. "Takes after his grandfather that way. Locked himself in the smokehouse for three days when we had our first real fight."

I don't know what to say to this unexpected visitor or her shared confidence.

"He showed me your review." Grace sits in the armchair by the window. "Beautiful writing. Honest."

"Thank you." The praise feels unearned.

"You love him." Not a question but a statement of fact.

"Yes." The truth rises in me, impossible to deny.

"And he loves you, though he's too angry to admit it right now."

"I betrayed his trust." Hope flickers, faint and dangerous.

"Yes, you did." Her bluntness is oddly comforting. "The question is, what matters more—being right or being happy?"

"I don't think it's that simple."

"It never is." She stands, smoothing her skirt. "I'm not here to offer easy forgiveness. That's Hunter's to give or withhold. But if you truly love my grandson, you'll fight for him. And if you don't think he's worth fighting for, then you should definitely get on that plane tomorrow."

She leaves as abruptly as she arrived, the door clicking softly behind her.

I sit on the edge of the bed, her words echoing in my mind. *Fight for him.*

The concept is foreign. I've spent my career fighting against mediocrity, against complacency, and against my fear of irrelevance. I've never fought for someone.

For connection.

For love.

The decision crystallizes slowly, certainty building like the gathering clouds outside my window. I'll leave tomorrow as planned. Give Hunter space.

But I won't disappear.

I'll write to him—not an email that is easily deleted or a text that is easily ignored, but a letter. Words on paper, honest and raw. And then another. And another. Until he knows the whole truth of what he means to me.

I pull out my laptop, open a document, and begin to write the first letter, not as the Executioner, but as Audrey.

Just Audrey.

My phone rings as I finish, an unknown local number. Probably the front desk confirming checkout details. I answer distractedly, still lost in the words I've written.

"Is this Audrey Tristan?" A familiar voice, though not Hunter's.

"Yes, this is Audrey."

"It's Miguel, Hunter's sous chef." His voice is low, urgent. "There's something you need to know. Lucas is replacing Hunter at Timberline."

The world shifts beneath me, pieces clicking into a terrible place. Lucas's eagerness about the review, his mention of "ideas" for capitalizing on the publicity, and the tension I'd sensed between the two men.

"What do you mean, replacing him?"

"Lucas thinks Timberline needs a more commercial chef now that it's getting national attention. Someone who'll create Instagram-worthy dishes, play to the crowds." Miguel's voice drips with disgust. "He's giving Hunter a choice—change his cooking style or step down."

"But the review celebrated Hunter's cooking exactly as it is." My stomach twists with the irony. The very success I helped create might cost Hunter everything.

"Lucas thinks your review creates an opportunity to 'elevate' the concept. Whatever that means."

"When is this happening?"

"Meeting tomorrow morning. Hunter doesn't know I'm calling you. He'd probably kill me if he did. But you got it right—in the review. About his food, about what makes this place special. And I thought..." Miguel hesitates. "I thought maybe you could help."

The request hangs between us, impossible and necessary all at once.

"I'll be there." The words come without conscious thought, certainty replacing hesitation. I'm not leaving Angel's Peak. Not yet.

I hang up and look at my half-packed suitcase. Slowly and deliberately, I return items to the drawers. The sweater. The dress. The shirt. Artifacts of a week that changed everything—and might yet lead somewhere after all.

Angel's Peak

CHAPTER 13

THE FIGHT

SLEEP EVADES ME ENTIRELY. I SPEND THE NIGHT crafting arguments and rehearsing speeches, and then discard them all as insufficient.

The truth is both simple and complicated: I love Hunter Morgan. I love how he touches herbs with reverence, the intensity in his eyes when he describes a dish, and the gentleness in his hands that belies their strength. I love the chef, the man, the soul beneath both. And I've hurt him in the worst possible way.

Dawn breaks over the mountains, painting my room in a golden light that feels undeserved. I dress carefully—jeans, boots, and a forest-green sweater that Hunter once said brought out flecks of gold in my eyes. Armor of a different sort than my usual city black.

The Haven stirs to life around me as I make my way downstairs. Staff members nod politely, unaware of yesterday's drama or too professional to acknowledge it. In the dining room, a small group is gathered outside the private meeting room—Lucas Reid's sanctum. Hunter stands among them, his back to me, shoulders rigid beneath his chef's jacket.

Miguel notices me first. His eyes widen in surprise and then relief. He tilts his head toward the meeting room door, silently telling me to step in.

"What's happening?" As I approach, I keep my voice low, directing the question to Miguel rather than risk Hunter's rejection.

"Lucas called a staff meeting. Said he has exciting news about Timberline's future." Miguel's expression says everything about what kind of "exciting" this news will be.

Hunter turns at the sound of my voice. The flash of emotion across his face is too complex to decipher—anger, yes, but something else beneath it. His eyes linger on my sweater for a heartbeat before his expression closes again.

"You're still here." Flat, uninflected.

"Had a change of plans." I hold his gaze, refusing to look away despite the discomfort pulsing between us.

"This is a private staff meeting." Each word is precisely enunciated, a chef's knife slicing through any pretense of civility.

"I invited her." Miguel straightens his spine, bracing for Hunter's reaction. "We need her."

Hunter's eyebrows draw together, betrayal freshly painted across his features. Before he can respond, the meeting room door swings open, and Lucas Reid emerges, expansive in his welcome.

"Everyone, please come in. It's an exciting day for Timberline." His gaze catches on me, surprise quickly masked by warmth. "Ms. Tristan, I didn't realize you were still in Angel's Peak. Please join us."

Hunter's jaw tightens, but he says nothing as we file into the room. A conference table dominates the space, and windows overlook the mountains that once seemed so promising to me. Now, they loom, impassive witnesses to whatever is about to unfold.

Lucas takes his position at the head of the table, tablet at the ready. Hunter remains standing while the rest of us—Miguel, the pastry chef, the sommelier, and two senior servers—take seats. I slide into a chair near the door, an outsider in every sense.

"First, I want to congratulate everyone on yesterday's review." Lucas beams with genuine pride. "The Executioner... uh, Audrey's stamp of approval is a game-changer for Timberline and The Haven. Reservations have tripled overnight."

Murmurs of excitement ripple through the staff. Only Hunter remains silent, arms crossed over his chest.

"This is our moment," Lucas continues. "Our opportunity to elevate Timberline to the next level. And I have some exciting new directions to discuss."

Here it comes. I lean forward, fingers pressed against the polished wood of the table.

"A restaurant group from Denver has approached me." Lucas swipes through his tablet. "They're interested in creating a partnership that would expand our reach. Pop-up dining experiences in major cities, a cookbook deal, possibly even a product line of signature sauces and spice blends."

The staff exchanges glances, uncertainty mixed with cautious interest.

"This would mean some adjustments to our concept, of course." Lucas's expression grows more serious. "More accessible menu items. Instagram-worthy presentations. Celebrity chef guest spots."

"You want to turn Timberline into a tourist trap." Hunter's voice cuts through the room like a blade, low but sharp.

Lucas meets Hunter's gaze steadily. "I want to capitalize on our success. The review praised your food, Hunter, but we must build on that foundation and create something with broader appeal."

"My food isn't a foundation for your franchise dreams. It's an expression of this place, these mountains, this community." Hunter's hands curl into fists at his sides, then deliberately relax. "We've discussed this before. My answer hasn't changed."

"The circumstances have." Lucas sets down his tablet, his expression grave. "The Haven is operating at a loss. You know this. Timberline is our only chance to turn things around, and I need a chef who understands the business reality."

The implied threat hangs in the air, clear to everyone present. My throat tightens as I watch the staff's expressions shift from excitement to concern.

"You're offering me an ultimatum." Hunter's voice remains steady. Tension coils in every line of his body. "Change my cooking or leave."

"I'm offering you an opportunity." Lucas leans forward. "One that many chefs would kill for. National exposure. Financial security. A chance to build something bigger than one restaurant in a town that most people couldn't find on a map."

"This town is my home." Simple words, profound in their conviction. "These people are my family. I returned to Angel's Peak to cook honest food that honors this place."

"Noble sentiments." Lucas's tone remains challenging. "But sentiments don't pay bills. The reality is that without changes, Timberline won't survive another year. Neither will The Haven."

"There are other ways to increase profitability without sacrificing our integrity." Hunter turns to Miguel. "The expansion plans we discussed—cooking classes, tasting menus featuring local producers, the winter foraging workshop series."

Miguel nods vigorously. "We've already had inquiries about all of those. People want authenticity, not gimmicks."

"People want whatever the market tells them to want."

Lucas dismisses this with a wave. "And right now, the market wants spectacle and social media moments."

"I disagree." The words leave my mouth before I can second-guess them.

All eyes turn to me, Hunter's most piercing of all.

"Ms. Tristan." Lucas's voice carries a warning. "While we appreciate your professional opinion, this is an internal business discussion."

"A discussion about the future of a restaurant I just reviewed." I straighten in my chair, drawing on every ounce of Executioner authority. "My readers didn't respond to Hunter's food because it was trendy or Instagram-worthy. They responded because it was honest, passionate, and deeply connected to this place."

Hunter's expression flickers with something—surprise, perhaps, or reluctant appreciation.

"With all due respect," Lucas's tone suggests none is actually due, "one positive review doesn't make you an expert on our business model."

"No, but fifteen years as a food critic does." I stand, mirroring Hunter's stance. "I've watched restaurants chase trends and lose their soul in the process. The most successful establishments—the ones with staying power—are those with a clear vision and the courage to stand by it."

"I'm not changing how I run my restaurant," Lucas says. "If you don't like it, find another chef who will do everything for you. I won't sacrifice the soul of Timberlake for a single dollar."

Lucas looks at me for a long moment, then at Hunter. Something shifts in his expression—not defeat, but a subtle transformation. He taps at his tablet, then sets it down decisively.

"And that," he says, his voice suddenly warm with approval, "is exactly the response I was hoping for."

The room goes still. Hunter's posture shifts minutely, confusion replacing anger.

"What?" he asks, the single word laden with suspicion.

Lucas's mouth curves into a genuine smile. "Hunter, when you brought me your vision for Timberline years ago, I believed in it completely. I still do. But after yesterday's review, we're going to be flooded with offers exactly like this one." He gestures to his tablet. "Some with much more money attached."

He stands, moving around the table to face the staff as a group rather than from a position of authority.

"I needed to know if success would change our vision. If the first sign of mainstream recognition would tempt us to compromise what makes Timberline special." He looks directly at Hunter. "I needed to hear you defend your food, this place, your community—not just to me, but to yourself and everyone in this room."

Understanding dawns on the faces around the table. Miguel lets out a soft laugh, shaking his head.

"You were testing us," he says.

"Not testing. Preparing." Lucas picks up his tablet again. "This offer is real. It came in at 6 AM. I've already drafted a refusal, but there will be others, and we need to be united in how we respond."

He swipes to a new screen and turns the tablet so we can all see. "This is what I want to discuss today: a business plan based on Hunter and Miguel's authentic expansion ideas— cooking classes, producer partnerships, and foraging work- shops. I've run the numbers, and with some adjustments, they're viable."

"You could have just said that from the beginning." Hunter's face remains guarded, but the rigid tension in his shoulders has eased.

"Would you have believed me if I hadn't shown you the

temptation first?" Lucas raises an eyebrow. "You're stubborn, Hunter. Sometimes you need to be pushed to articulate why you believe in something so strongly."

"You're manipulative," Hunter retorts, but there's less heat in it now.

"I'm strategic," Lucas corrects, not unkindly. "And I've been protecting your vision from corporate vultures since we opened. But after yesterday's review..." His expression sobers. "The stakes are higher now. The Haven can't survive as it is. That part wasn't a test. We need Timberline to succeed, but on our terms, not theirs."

He turns to the rest of the staff. "I wanted everyone to hear Hunter's passionate defense of what makes this place special. That's the North Star we follow, no matter how tempting other offers might be."

Relief and renewed excitement ripple through the room. Hunter's expression remains guarded, but I can see him reassessing, recalculating.

"Then let me invest." The offer still surprises me, but once spoken, it feels inevitable. "I have savings. Enough to buy a stake in Timberline and help fund Hunter's expansion ideas."

Shock ripples through the room. Hunter's eyes widen, his carefully constructed mask slipping.

"You would invest in a restaurant run by a chef who currently hates you?" Lucas asks, but his incredulity seems more curious than dismissive.

I look directly at Hunter. "I believe in his vision. In what he's building here. Whether or not he forgives me is irrelevant to that fact. You need capital, and I have that."

For a heartbeat, the room falls silent. I can almost see Hunter's thoughts racing behind his eyes—suspicion, confusion, calculation.

"I need to speak with Ms. Tristan. Alone." Hunter's voice

leaves no room for argument. "The rest of you, give us the room."

Lucas exchanges a look with Hunter I can't quite decipher —something like understanding passing between them— before nodding.

"Of course." He gathers his tablet and gestures to the others. "Let's give them space."

Lucas ushers the staff out, closing the door firmly behind them.

Hunter and I stand facing each other across the conference table, the mountains bearing silent witness through the windows.

"What are you doing?" Exhaustion threads through the anger in his voice.

"Trying to fix what I broke." My hands tremble, and I press them flat against the table to steady them. "Or, at least, not make it worse."

"By throwing money at the problem? Buying your way into my restaurant after betraying my trust?" His words sting, but there's more weariness than venom in them now.

"No. By believing in you. In what you've built here." I take a breath, searching for words worthy of this moment. "I didn't lie in the review. Every word was true. Your food moved me. Not because we slept together, but because you cook with your whole heart. It's the most honest thing I've experienced in years."

He paces the length of the windows, fingers raking through his hair. "You have no idea what you're offering. Restaurants are money pits. Especially ones like Timberline."

"I know exactly what I'm offering." I stand my ground. "A chance to preserve what makes this place special."

"Why?" He stops, turning to face me fully. "Why would you do this?"

The question I've been waiting for. The one that matters most.

"Because I fell in love with Angel's Peak." I take a step toward him, then another. "With the mountains, the town, and the greenhouse where we first met. With your grandfather's trout recipe and how you talked about wild mushrooms. With the look on your face when you described the perfect dish." Another step. "But mostly, Hunter, I fell in love with you, and because Eleanor said I needed to fight for what I love."

The words hang between us, honest, raw, and terrifying in their vulnerability. Hunter remains motionless, his expression unreadable.

"You lied to me." Not an accusation this time, but a statement of fact.

"Yes. I will regret that every day." I don't try to justify or explain away the hurt I've caused. "I came to Angel's Peak as The Executioner, looking for a story. I'm staying as Audrey if you'll let me."

Hunter crosses his arms, studying me with the intensity he usually reserves for ingredients he's not sure how to use. "And if I don't accept your investment? If I tell you to leave?"

My heart contracts painfully, but I lift my chin. "Then I'll go. But I'll still fight for what you've built here. Write follow-up articles. Send other critics. Make sure the world knows what's happening in this kitchen on this mountain."

"Why should I trust anything you say now?" The question is fair, devastating in its simplicity.

"You shouldn't." The admission costs me. "Trust has to be earned back. I'm asking for the chance to earn it."

Silence stretches between us, taut as a wire. Outside, clouds gather around the mountain peaks, shadows racing across the valley below.

"I need time." Hunter moves toward the door, pausing

with his hand on the knob. "To think. To decide what Timberline means to me, what I'm willing to sacrifice for it."

"I understand." I remain where I am, afraid any movement might shatter this fragile moment.

"Stay in Angel's Peak." It is neither a request nor a command. "Until I make my decision."

"I will." Hope blooms, tender, and cautious.

He nods once, then leaves, the door clicking quietly behind him.

Alone in the conference room, I sink into a chair, legs suddenly unable to support me. I watch Hunter walk across the property through the windows toward the greenhouse.

Our beginning.

Perhaps still our middle, if not yet our end.

My phone buzzes with a text from Miguel: *Well?*

I type back simply: *He's thinking. I'm staying.*

The response comes immediately: *Good. He thinks too much. Stubborn bastard.*

Despite everything, a laugh escapes me. This small moment of connection with someone who cares for Hunter as much as I do feels like a lifeline.

Outside, the gathering clouds finally break, rain sheeting down against the windows. I watch as Hunter reaches the greenhouse door, hesitates, then enters. Even from this distance, the weight of difficult decisions sits heavily on his shoulders.

My phone buzzes again. This time, it's my editor: *Readers are going crazy for your review. I need a follow-up piece ASAP. What's the angle?*

I consider the question, watching Hunter's silhouette move among the plants we both love. The angle. Always the angle in my world of words and assessments. However, the story here is no longer about food. It's about roots and growth and the courage it takes to plant something new.

I type back: *The angle is Transformation. Give me a week.*

Then I slip my phone into my pocket and go to the door. The rain eases to a gentle patter. Hunter is deciding our fate in that greenhouse.

All I can do now is wait, hope, and remember why I came to Angel's Peak in the first place—to find a story worth telling.

And perhaps, if I'm very lucky, a love worth fighting for.

Angel's Peak

CHAPTER 14

PERFECT PAIRING

THE MAGAZINE ARRIVES VIA COURIER WHILE I'M having coffee at Maggie's Diner, staring out at the mountains as if they might offer some wisdom about Hunter's silence over the past three days. The delivery man checks my ID twice before handing over the thick padded envelope.

"Special delivery from New York," he says, curiosity evident in his tone. Small towns and their insatiable appetite for gossip.

I tear it open, coffee forgotten as I pull out the glossy publication. My breath catches. Timberline dominates the cover—Hunter's hands preparing the mountain trout, steam rising from the cast iron pan, a dusting of pine ash visible on the wooden cutting board.

The headline reads: *"Mountain Magic: The Hidden Culinary Gem That's Changing Destination Dining."*

But it's the smaller text at the bottom that makes my heart stutter: *"Plus: Chef Morgan's Grandfather's Secret Trout Recipe - A Taste of Heritage."*

The recipe—the one Hunter taught me during our private

cooking lesson—is the one I'd written up and sent to my editor as potential companion content to my review, never imagining she'd feature it so prominently.

"Oh no." The words escape in a whisper.

Darlene glances over as she refills my mug. "Bad news, honey?"

"I need to go." I throw bills on the counter, gathering my things in frantic motion. "Now."

The drive to Timberline takes seven minutes. It feels like seven hours. My mind races through scenarios, each worse than the last. Hunter seeing this as fresh betrayal. The fragile trust we'd begun rebuilding shattered beyond repair. His grandfather's cherished recipe exposed without permission.

The parking lot is filled to capacity, and a line of people waits outside the restaurant's entrance. My review and now this magazine feature have done exactly what Lucas wanted—brought attention—but at what cost?

I push through the crowd, ignoring the irritated murmurs as I bypass the line. The dining room is packed to capacity, servers weaving between the tables. A hostess I don't recognize holds a tablet at the entrance, managing the growing waitlist.

"I need to see Hunter." My voice sounds breathless, even to my ears. "It's important."

She gives me the sympathetic but firm look of someone who's heard every possible line to skip the wait. "Chef Morgan is extremely busy. If you'd like to leave your name—"

"Tell him it's Audrey. About the magazine."

Something in my expression must convey my desperation because she hesitates and then nods,

"Wait here."

Minutes stretch like taffy, sticky and uncomfortable. Through the restaurant's windows, I watch the orchestrated chaos of a successful dinner service. Miguel expedites at the pass. Line cooks move in synch. And Hunter—focused, commanding, calling orders with the authority of a general on the battlefield.

The magazine feels heavy in my hands, evidence of another mistake I never intended to make.

The hostess returns, expression carefully neutral. "Chef Morgan can spare a moment. Follow me."

She leads me through the packed dining room. Diners turn to stare, some recognizing me from my byline photo, others simply curious about who rates special treatment. Near the kitchen entrance, Lucas Reid speaks animatedly with what appears to be a potential investor, his gestures expansive, face flushed with unexpected success.

The hostess shows me to Hunter's small office, a converted storage room adjacent to the kitchen. "He'll be with you shortly."

Alone, I examine the tiny space that holds pieces of Hunter's soul. Framed photos of his grandparents. Sketches for seasonal menu items. A shelf of well-worn cookbooks, spines cracked from frequent use. A small potted herb—thyme—growing beneath a desk lamp.

The door opens, and Hunter enters, chef's jacket spotted with the evidence of service, face lined with exhaustion but eyes bright with the adrenaline of a successful night.

"Audrey." My name on his lips sends electricity down my spine, even when weighed with wariness.

"I'm sorry." I thrust the magazine toward him like a confession. "I didn't know they would publish this. I sent it as background material for my editor, not for publication. Especially not like this."

He takes it and studies the cover silently. His expression reveals nothing as he flips to the article, scanning the pages with the efficiency of someone used to reading recipes at a glance.

"I would never have shared your grandfather's recipe without permission." The words tumble out, desperate and sincere. "I know what it means to you. How personal it is."

Hunter closes the magazine and sets it on his cluttered desk. The silence stretches between us, unbearable in its weight.

"They spelled my grandfather's name correctly."

Of all the responses I anticipated, that isn't one of them. "What?"

"Here." He reopens the magazine and points to the introduction of the recipe. "They got it right. Charles Morgan. Most publications butcher it somehow. Make him Charles Moran or Charlie Morgan."

I stare at him, struggling to read his reaction. "You're not angry?"

A laugh escapes him, short and surprised. "About the magazine? No." He runs a hand through his hair, leaving it standing on end. "About you leaving town without saying goodbye? Yes."

"Leaving?" My confusion is genuine. "I'm not leaving."

"Miguel said you checked out of The Haven this morning."

Understanding dawns. "I moved to Mabel's guest house. The Haven was getting... expensive."

Something shifts in Hunter's expression, a tension releasing. "So you're staying in Angel's Peak."

"Until you tell me to go." The admission costs me nothing; it's simply the truth. "You did tell me to stay. Or did I get that wrong?"

He studies me for a long moment, and his chef's assessment turns personal.

"The restaurant's insane tonight. Completely booked through the next two weeks. The phone hasn't stopped ringing."

"I noticed." I gesture toward the packed dining room beyond his door.

"Lucas is beside himself. He's had three different investor groups approach him today alone." A wry smile touches Hunter's lips. "Suddenly, my 'unmarketable' cooking style seems very marketable indeed."

Hope flutters in my chest, a tentative wing-beat. "That's good, right? For Timberline, for your vision?"

"It is." He steps closer, close enough that I can smell the kitchen on him—herbs, smoke, and the particular aroma that belongs only to Hunter. "But there's something I need to know first."

My heart hammers against my ribs. "Anything."

"Why did you submit that particular recipe to your editor?"

It's an unexpected question, but one I can answer honestly.

"Because it was perfect. It captured everything special about your cooking—respect for ingredients, connection to place, and technique in service of flavor rather than ego. Because..." I hesitate, then commit to honesty "because it reminds me of you."

He nods slowly as if confirming something to himself. "I need to get back to service. But afterward, can we talk?"

"Yes." The single syllable carries the weight of promises I intend to keep.

"Wait in the greenhouse. I'll find you when we're done."

Night transforms the greenhouse; moonlight filters through the glass to create patterns across the earthen floor. I move among the herbs and seedlings, brushing my fingers across lemon thyme and rosemary, the precious alpine varietals Hunter cultivates with such care.

Two hours pass before the door opens. Hunter enters,

changed from his chef's whites into jeans and a soft flannel shirt, looking less armored.

"Sorry for the wait. Had to make sure Miguel had everything under control."

"It's fine. I've been keeping your plants company."

He smiles at that, a genuine smile that reaches his eyes. "They're good listeners. No judgment."

"Unlike food critics?" The self-deprecating joke slips out before I can reconsider.

"Some critics." He moves closer, stopping at the wooden workbench where this all began, where we first touched. "I wanted to thank you."

"For what?"

"The recipe credit. You made sure my grandfather's contribution was acknowledged. That matters to me."

I nod, throat tight with unexpected emotion. "His legacy deserves recognition."

"It does." Hunter studies me, eyes reflecting the moonlight streaming through glass panels.

"I love this place. What you've built here." I swallow hard, gathering courage. "I love *you*."

The admission hangs between us, fragile as a soap bubble, iridescent with hope.

"I've been afraid to trust again." His voice drops, intimate as a confessional. "My ex-partner didn't just steal recipes. He took my confidence. He made me question my judgment, especially about people."

"I understand." And I do. The particular agony of trusting wrongly and the scars it leaves behind.

"But I've been thinking about something my grandmother said." He steps closer, close enough that I can see the fine lines around his eyes, evidence of laughter and sun. "About the difference between heat and warmth."

I wait, letting him find his way to whatever truth he discovered.

"Heat is instant. Intense. It burns bright but can cause damage if you're not careful." His hand lifts and hovers near my face without touching it. "Warmth sustains. Nurtures. Lasts through cold seasons."

My breath catches, hope expanding in my chest like bread dough in a warm kitchen.

"What we had that first night in the greenhouse was heat." His eyes don't leave mine. "What we built over the following days, cooking together, foraging, talking—that was the beginning of genuine warmth. The kind that can last if we let it."

"Hunter—" His name emerges half-whisper, half-prayer.

"I'm not ready to throw that away. No matter how it started." His fingers finally make contact, brushing a strand of hair from my face. "The local investment group made an offer. Partnership in Timberline. Creative control for me, financial backing from them."

"That's wonderful." The words emerge heartfelt but weighted with uncertainty about what this means for us.

"It is. It means I can stay true to my vision. To my grandfather's legacy." His hand cups my cheek now, warm and certain. "But success feels hollow without someone to share it with. Someone who understands both the food and the man behind it."

My heart stutters and restarts. "What are you saying?"

"I want honesty between us. No more secrets. No more professional masks." His thumb traces my lower lip, feather-light. "Can you give me that?"

"Yes." No hesitation, no qualification. "I've been thinking about changes, too. My editor wants me to consider a culinary travel series. Something deeper than reviews—stories about chefs and communities and food traditions. Starting with mountain cuisine."

A smile touches his lips. "Sounds like something you'd be good at."

"It would mean less time being The Executioner. More time being Audrey."

"I like Audrey." His smile deepens. "I love her."

The words break something open inside me, joy rushing in like spring thaw. "I want nothing more than to stay here with you."

His lips find mine, gentle at first, then with growing intensity. Not the desperate heat of our first encounter but something deeper—passion tempered with tenderness, desire woven with emerging love. His hands cradle my face as if I'm something precious, something worth protecting.

"Stay in Angel's Peak." When we part, breathless, he rests his forehead against mine.

"For how long?" I need to hear him say it.

"For good." His voice holds certainty, the same confidence he brings to creating perfect dishes. "Build your new career here. With me."

"My work will take me away sometimes. Your hours are impossible. We're both stubborn and driven and—"

He silences me with another kiss, brief but effective. "We're also creative problem-solvers. We'll figure it out."

At this moment, in this greenhouse where we began, surrounded by growing things that require patience and care, I believe him. I believe in us—not as a perfect pairing but as ingredients that complement each other, creating something better together than apart.

"I'd like that very much." I wind my arms around his neck, drawing him closer.

His smile curves—wicked, knowing. "Good. You move in with me tonight."

"Tonight?" My laugh catches in my throat. "That's a bit presumptuous."

"It's what's going to happen." His hands skim down to my hips, fingers flexing. "I want you in my bed. On your knees. Tied to the posts. Completely at my mercy."

Heat licks up my spine.

"But first..." His voice dips lower, rougher. "We're going to talk. About limits. About control. About what this really looks like."

My pulse thrums. "And after?"

"After," he murmurs, brushing his lips over my ear, "I'm going to punish you."

"Punish me?" I still. Not from fear—anticipation coils deep and tight.

"For lying to me," he continues, his tone harder now. "For looking me in the eye and pretending you were just some tourist. For letting me touch you without knowing who you really were."

My mouth opens to speak, to defend—but he presses a thumb to my lips.

"You're mine now," he growls. "And being mine means honesty. No more games. You accept your punishment. We wipe the slate clean."

"I'm sorry." I nod, throat tight.

"You will be." His eyes soften, but only slightly.

The promise in his voice is pure sin.

"Tonight, I'm going to make you feel every bit of what you denied me. I'll take my time stripping that control from you, inch by inch, until all that's left is the truth. Your truth. My hands. Your pleasure."

"Yes, Chef." A shudder rolls through me.

He smirks. "Say that again when I've got you begging."

"You planning to ruin me?" I grin, already breathless.

"Oh, sweetheart," he says, mouth brushing mine. "I plan to ruin you, own you, and cook you a gourmet breakfast after."

I bite my lower lip, heart pounding.

His mouth brushes my ear.

"Then I'll start again."

God help me, I can't wait. I want this man. His town. This life.

"I hope you like a challenge," I murmur. "I can be quite ornery."

"That's okay. I like a challenge." His grin is pure promise. "You're mine now."

And just like that, I am.

Utterly.

Deliciously.

Irrevocably his.

———

SIX MONTHS LATER, THE CAMERA CREW ADJUSTS THE lighting as I prepare to film the opening segment of "Roots & Routes," my new culinary travel series.

Behind me, Timberline gleams, transformed but true to Hunter's vision—expanded kitchen, additional greenhouse, cooking school under construction.

Hunter watches from behind the producer, arms crossed over his chest, pride evident in every line of his body. When our eyes meet, he winks, a private communication in a public moment.

"Ready in five, four, three..." The producer counts down silently with fingers for the final numbers.

I take a breath, centering myself in this new role and life we're building.

"Welcome to Angel's Peak, where a hidden culinary gem is redefining destination dining through its connection to place, tradition, and the vision of one remarkable chef..."

The words flow easily and authentically. Because this isn't

a story I'm telling—it's a story I'm *living*. With Hunter. With this community. With the mountains that called us both home.

As the camera pans to capture Hunter approaching to demonstrate his grandfather's famous trout recipe, his hand briefly finds mine off-camera, a touch that carries all the warmth we've built together.

We've found the perfect pairing, at last.

Angel's Peak

CHAPTER 15

THE PERFECT BLEND

ANGEL'S PEAK IN AUTUMN IS A PAINTER'S DREAM—mountains ablaze with sunset colors; aspen leaves shimmering gold against evergreen, and the first dusting of snow on the highest peaks.

Standing at the kitchen window of the expanded Timberline, I pause to absorb the view that still takes my breath away, even after a year of waking to it daily.

"Admiring the scenery when we have prep to finish?" Hunter's voice carries no real reproach, only the comfortable teasing of partners who've found their rhythm.

"Inspiration." I turn to face him, warmth blooming in my chest at the sight of him in his element—sleeves rolled to reveal strong forearms dusted with flour, confidence in every movement as he expertly crimps dough. "Some of us need it for creative work."

"And some of us need to finish these tarts before two hundred guests arrive." But he smiles, the crinkles around his eyes deepening in the way I've come to treasure.

The kitchen around us bustles with focused energy. Student chefs from the newly established Mountain Culinary

Institute—Timberline's educational offshoot—move with purpose under Miguel's watchful eye.

What began as Hunter's dream of teaching traditional mountain cooking techniques has blossomed into a prestigious program with a waiting list two years long.

I move to my station, adjusting the camera setup for today's special episode of "Roots & Routes."

My culinary travel series has found its audience—people hungry for recipes and the stories behind them. The network initially balked at my insistence on keeping Angel's Peak as my home base rather than relocating to New York, but the authenticity of filming where the food traditions live has become the show's trademark.

"How's the special sauce coming along?" Hunter appears beside me, sampling a spoonful of the pine-infused reduction I've been working on. His eyes close briefly in appreciation. "Perfect. Like everything you do."

"Flatterer." I bump his hip with mine, the casual intimacy between us now as natural as breathing. "You just want me to help with those tarts."

"Maybe." His hand finds the small of my back, warm through the fabric of my chef's whites. "Or maybe I just want an excuse to stand close to my almost-wife."

Almost-wife. The words still thrill me, even after months of engagement. Today—finally—I'll become Hunter Morgan's wife, and our journey from that first heated greenhouse encounter to partnership is complete in every sense.

The greenhouse.

Now transformed into the region's most sought-after private dining space, the glass-walled structure connects to Timberline by a covered walkway. We've preserved its original character while adding heat for winter, cooling for summer, and a single table that seats twenty beneath a canopy of climbing herbs and edible flowers.

Tonight, it will host our wedding reception after a sunset ceremony at Lookout Point.

"There's my favorite culinary power couple." Eleanor Morgan's voice precedes her into the kitchen, her diminutive frame carrying the authority of someone who's been feeding people for seven decades. Hunter's grandmother has become my fiercest champion and gentlest critic. "You two planning to cook through your own wedding?"

"Just finishing prep, Gran." Hunter drops a kiss on her weathered cheek. "Everything under control."

"So I see." She casts an expert eye over the organized chaos, nodding approval at the *mise en place*. "Remember when you couldn't boil water without burning it, Hunter James Morgan?"

"I was four, Gran."

"And stubborn as a mule even then." She winks at me. "Some things never change."

"Thank goodness for that." I accept her hug, breathing in the scent of lavender that always clings to her. "His stubbornness is why we're still here."

"That and your persistence." She pats my cheek affectionately. "Now, I'm going to supervise the flower arrangements because Lord knows those city florists have no idea what mountain blooms look like."

We watch her march determinedly toward the dining room, staff parting before her like the Red Sea.

"Hurricane Eleanor strikes again." Hunter slides an arm around my waist. "Poor florists don't stand a chance."

"Neither did we." I lean into him briefly before returning to work.

We move in tandem, anticipating each other's needs, passing utensils before they're requested, tasting and adjusting each other's creations with the synchronicity that comes from a year of cooking side by side.

The kitchen doors swing open to admit Lucas Reid, Hunter's most determined ally. Under our culinary influence, and one spectacular wedding of the century, the Haven has become the region's premier destination, booked solid year-round.

"Chef." Lucas nods at Hunter, then me. "Final walk-through complete. Everything's ready for tonight."

"Any issues?" Hunter hands me a spoonful of sauce to taste.

"Nothing our grandmother hasn't already identified and corrected." Lucas's dry tone hints at his humor. "I think she's arranged additional seating for the Johnson twins from the bakery."

"They're bringing the bread." I add a pinch of salt to the sauce and offer it back to Hunter for approval. "We can't have our bread suppliers sitting in the back."

"Of course not." Lucas glances at his watch. "Four hours until ceremony time. The kitchen seems ahead of schedule."

"We've got this." Hunter's confidence isn't bravado but earned certainty. "Go check on the bar setup. Mabel's bringing her homemade elderberry liqueur for the welcome cocktail."

Lucas departs, already tapping notes into his ever-present tablet.

"He's almost human these days." I seal containers of prepped ingredients, labeling each with precise instructions.

"Success will do that." Hunter moves behind me, arms circling my waist as he rests his chin on my shoulder. "That, and the perfect woman."

I pause, arching a brow.

"Amelia pulled off the wedding of the century in the middle of a blizzard, single-handedly putting The Haven on the national map. Premier wedding and food destination, thanks to her, and she managed to put a spring in his step..."

"And you?"

He presses a kiss just below my ear. "I found mine in a greenhouse, challenging my authority and blowing up my world one review at a time."

A smile tugs at my lips.

"Speaking of which," he murmurs, "your show's ratings came in..."

"And?"

"Highest of the season. The network called while you were at the fitting. They're offering a three-year renewal with an increased production budget."

I turn in his arms, searching his face. "That means more travel. More time away from Angel's Peak. From you."

"Or more reason to come with you." His hands settle at my waist, thumbs tracing small circles. "Part-time, at least. Miguel can handle Timberline for stretches. The students would benefit from international perspectives."

"You'd do that?" The question emerges softly with wonder.

"We're partners, Audrey. In life, in business, in everything that matters." His forehead rests against mine. "Besides, I hear there are mountains with interesting culinary traditions all over the world."

"I love you." The words still feel new each time I say them, bright as fresh herbs.

"Good thing, since you're marrying me in a few hours." His smile turns playful. "Unless you're having second thoughts?"

"Not a chance, Chef Morgan." I rise on tiptoe to press a brief kiss to his lips. "I know a perfect pairing when I taste one."

The rest of the afternoon passes in a blur of activity. Mabel arrives with her famous liqueur, stopping to fuss over how thin she thinks I look despite a year of Angel's Peak cooking. Jackson Hart brings wild mushrooms he foraged at dawn, a wedding gift he insists on incorporating into the menu himself. Maggie from the diner delivers her special blend of coffee beans, roasted precisely for our dessert course. Amelia, my wedding planner, runs around making sure everything is perfect and on track.

In the midst of this beautiful chaos, I find myself alone in the greenhouse for a stolen moment of quiet. The space has been transformed for tonight—tiny lights woven through herb trellises, the long table set with vintage china Hunter's grandmother contributed, each place marked with a hand-written card detailing the guest's connection to our story.

At the far end, partially hidden behind mature rosemary plants, sits a new addition: a small nursery section with tiny seedlings in miniature pots—baby herbs, as Hunter calls them—each one labeled with care and protected by specialized glass to maintain its perfect growing environment.

My hand drifts unconsciously to my stomach. The secret I've been keeping for three weeks, waiting for the perfect moment to share with Hunter.

"There you are." His voice draws me from contemplation. "The team's looking for final approval on the amuse-bouche plating."

"It's beautiful in here." I turn to face him, taking in how handsome he looks even in work clothes, his presence still capable of quickening my pulse after all this time. "Everything we dreamed."

He crosses to me, eyes softening as he registers my mood. "Second thoughts after all?"

"The opposite." I take his hands in mine, drawing him to the nursery section. "I added something to our greenhouse. A new project."

His brow furrows as he examines the careful setup, the tiny seedlings breaking through the soil.

"Baby herbs? I thought we were waiting until after the expansion to start the rare varietals program."

"These aren't just any seedlings." I guide his hand to my abdomen, watching comprehension dawn in his eyes. "These are symbolic ones. For our own little seedling."

Time suspends as he processes my meaning, his expression transforming from confusion to wonder to incandescent joy.

"You're pregnant?" The words emerge in a whisper, reverent and awed.

I nod, tears blurring my vision. "About eight weeks. Our own little sous chef in training."

His arms enfold me with tender urgency, his face buried in my hair. When he pulls back, his cheeks are damp. "A baby. Our baby."

"Due in spring. When everything begins growing again."

Hunter drops to his knees, hands framing my stomach with exquisite gentleness as if I've suddenly become infinitely precious.

"Hello in there, little one. I'm your dad." His voice breaks on the last word. "And I already love you more than I thought possible."

The moment is so pure and perfect that I want to preserve it forever. This man—my almost-husband, soon-to-be father of my child—kneeling before me in the greenhouse where our story began, making his first promises to our future.

He stands, cradling my face in his hands. "When were you going to tell me?"

"Tonight. After the reception. As our private celebration." I cover his hands with mine. "But this moment felt right. Here, where everything began for us."

"It's perfect." He kisses me with such tenderness that it makes my heart ache. "Everything is perfect."

"Chef? Audrey?" Miguel's voice calls from the walkway.

"Sorry to interrupt, but we need final decisions on the wine pairings."

Reality intrudes, but gently. Hunter's hand finds mine, squeezing once before releasing. "We should get back."

"Wait." I pull him back for one more moment of privacy. "Let's exchange our private vows now. Just us, before the formal ceremony."

His expression softens with understanding. "Yes."

In the golden afternoon, light filters through glass walls, and we are surrounded by growing things that have witnessed our journey from strangers to lovers to partners. We face each other with joined hands.

"Hunter Morgan." My voice steadies as I find the words I've rehearsed in my heart. "I promise to approach our life together with the same care you bring to your cooking—attention to detail, respect for tradition, and courage to innovate. I promise honesty in all things, passion in both work and love, and partnership in every challenge. I promise to remind you of your worth when doubt creeps in, to celebrate your triumphs, and to build something lasting with you, day by day, season by season."

His thumbs brush away tears I hadn't realized were falling. When he speaks, his voice carries the weight of absolute certainty.

"Audrey Tristan Morgan." The name I'll bear after today already sounds right on his lips. "I promise to nurture our life together with the patience I bring to cultivating rare herbs—creating perfect conditions for growth, protecting what's precious, and savoring the fruits of our combined labor. I promise transparency where once I built walls, commitment where once I kept distance, and unwavering support as you pursue your dreams. I promise to see you—truly see you—every day of our lives together, to listen when words fail, and to build a legacy worthy of passing to our children."

He places a hand gently on my stomach at these last words, the promise extending now to the tiny life we've created together.

Our lips meet in a kiss that seals these private vows, a perfect blend of passion and tenderness, heat and warmth, present joy and future promise.

"I love you," he whispers against my lips. "Both of you."

"And we love you." The plural feels strange and wonderful on my tongue.

Amelia appears at the greenhouse entrance, apologetic but insistent. "Thirty minutes until you both need to get changed for the ceremony."

Reality beckons once more. With a final kiss, we return to the controlled chaos of wedding preparations. The ceremony at Lookout Point unfolds exactly as planned, the late afternoon sun bathing Angel's Peak in golden light as we exchange our formal vows before friends, family, and the entire town that has become our home.

At the reception, champagne flows and plates emerge from the kitchen in perfect succession, each dish telling part of our story—from the pine-smoked trout that first captured my professional admiration to the alpine herb salad harvested from our greenhouse.

When the time comes for dessert, I signal the kitchen staff to wait. Standing beside Hunter at the head of the table, I raise my water glass.

"As some of you may have noticed, I'm not joining in the champagne toasts tonight." Murmurs ripple through the gathering. "We have a special dessert announcement."

Hunter's arm slides around my waist, his smile radiant as I place his hand over my abdomen.

"We're expecting." The words ring out clear and joyful. "Our own little sous chef arrives in spring."

The greenhouse erupts in cheers, Eleanor Morgan's voice rising above the rest as she declares she "knew it all along." Jackson Hart slaps Hunter on the back with such enthusiasm that he nearly topples a centerpiece. Maggie from the diner immediately offers to supply special pregnancy-safe herbal teas. Even Lucas Reid appears genuinely moved, offering sincere congratulations.

Later, after the last guest has departed and the kitchen staff has completed cleanup, Hunter and I find ourselves alone in the greenhouse once more. He pours us tea from the pot Maggie insisted on leaving, and we settle on the small bench near the seedling nursery.

"So, Mrs. Morgan." The name sounds like a caress from his lips. "What next for our little empire?"

I nestle against his side, content beyond words. "The culinary school expansion. Your cookbook. Season three of the show. This little one." My hand rests on my stomach. "Plenty to keep us busy."

"And after that?" His arm tightens around me. "What's the five-year plan?"

I smile at his need to plan ahead and map the future as precisely as a recipe. "Maybe a sister restaurant in Aspen? Or that teaching kitchen for underprivileged kids you've been talking about?"

"All of it." He presses a kiss to my temple. "With you beside me, I want all of it."

The greenhouse settles around us, glass walls now containing far more than herbs and vegetables. They hold our beginning, our present, and our future—all the secret ingredients that transformed a one-night encounter into a lifetime commitment.

Hunter lifts his teacup in a toast. "To the unexpected ingredients."

I clink my cup against his. "And the perfect blend they created."

Outside, the first stars appear above Angel's Peak, witnesses to promises kept and dreams taking root. Inside, wrapped in the warmth of Hunter's embrace, I've never felt more certain of anything in my life.

This—us—is the recipe I've been searching for all along.

***

Love the heat in Angel's Peak?

If you're enjoying all the steamy, small-town instalove stories this mountain town has to offer, you're going to fall hard for Trapped with the Forest Ranger

This next swoon-worthy romance serves up spice, sweetness, and a hero who knows exactly what he wants—*her*.

Click here to dive into Trapped with the Forest Ranger

***

When wildlife photographer Harper Wells gets caught in a mountain storm, she never expects to find shelter—or salvation—with the brooding forest ranger who reluctantly takes her in.

Caleb Donovan has spent three years in self-imposed isolation on Angel's Peak, haunted by the wildfire that claimed his fiancée and ended his firefighting career. The last thing he needs is a stubborn, city-bred photographer tracking mud through his perfectly ordered sanctuary.

But as days turn into nights and the storm rages on, the walls between them crumble. Harper sees past his gruff exterior to the wounded protector beneath, while Caleb discovers a woman as untamed as the wilderness he guards. When forced proximity ignites into explosive passion, neither can deny the primal hunger consuming them.

Just as Harper begins to imagine a life beyond constant motion, a career-defining opportunity threatens to tear them apart.

Can love born in isolation survive the real world? Or will their fierce connection be just another casualty of the storm?

A steamy instalove romance featuring a damaged alpha hero, a determined heroine, and the healing power of wild passion in the untamed wilderness.

➡️ Click here to dive into Trapped with the Forest Ranger

Featuring the TROPES you LOVE

🏔️ FORCED PROXIMITY - STRANDED TOGETHER during mountain storms

🔥 Grumpy/Sunshine - Brooding ranger meets spirited photographer

💔 Wounded Hero - Haunted by tragic past, rebuilt by love

⚡ Instalove - Instant attraction that deepens into forever love

🌲 Wilderness Romance - Passion ignites in pristine mountain setting

🎯 Opposites Attract - Nomadic adventurer vs. rooted protector

💪 Alpha Hero - Dominant, protective, utterly devoted

🔥 Steamy Romance - Explosive chemistry and passionate encounters

💕 Found Family - Building home together in the wilderness

Career vs Love - Choosing between dreams and destiny

Shared Purpose - Wildlife conservation brings them together

Home is Where the Heart Is - Finding belonging in unexpected places

Click here to dive into Trapped with the Forest Ranger

Angel's Peak

Please consider leaving a review

I hope you enjoyed this book as much as I enjoyed writing it. If you like this book, please leave a review. I love reviews. I love reading your reviews, and they help other readers decide if this book is worth their time and money. I hope you think it is and decide to share this story with others. A sentence is all it takes. Thank you in advance!

CLICK ON THE LINK BELOW TO LEAVE YOUR REVIEW
Goodreads
Amazon
Bookbub

Angel's Peak

ELLZ BELLZ

Ellie's Facebook Reader Group

If you are interested in joining the ELLZ BELLZ, Ellie's Facebook reader group, we'd love to have you.

Join Ellie's ELLZ BELLZ.
The ELLZ BELLZ Facebook Reader Group

Sign up for Ellie's Newsletter.
Elliemasters.com/newslettersignup

Also by Ellie Masters

The LIGHTER SIDE

Ellie Masters is the lighter side of the Jet & Ellie Masters writing duo! You will find Contemporary Romance, Military Romance, Romantic Suspense, Billionaire Romance, and Rock Star Romance in Ellie's Works.

YOU CAN FIND ELLIE'S BOOKS HERE:

ELLIEMASTERS.COM/BOOKS

SUGGESTED READING ORDER

START HERE

Rockstar Romance

The Angel Fire Rock Romance Series

EACH BOOK IN THIS SERIES CAN BE READ AS A STANDALONE AND IS ABOUT A DIFFERENT COUPLE WITH AN HEA. IT IS RECOMMENDED THEY ARE READ IN ORDER.

Heart's Insanity

Ashes to New

Heart's Desire

Heart's Collide

Hearts Divided

Hearts Entwined

Forest's FALL

Hearts The Last Beat

CONTINUE HERE...

__Military Romance__
__Guardian Hostage Rescue Specialists__
Rescuing Melissa
*(*Get a FREE copy of Rescuing Melissa
when you join Ellie's Newsletter*)*

Alpha Team

Rescuing Zoe

Rescuing Moira

Rescuing Eve

Rescuing Lily

Rescuing Jinx

Rescuing Maria

Bravo Team

Rescuing Angie

Rescuing Isabelle

Rescuing Carmen

Rescuing Rosalie

Rescuing Kaye

Cara's Protector

Rescuing Barbi

Charlie Team

Rescuing Rebel

Rescuing Stitch

Rescuing Mia

Jenna's Protector

Rescuing Sophia

Rescuing Malia

Rescuing Ally (Part 1)

Rescuing Ally (Part 2)

Delta Team

Rescuing Ember

Rescuing Aria

STANDALONES IN THE GUARDIAN HOSTAGE RESCUE SERIES YOU CAN READ ANYTIME

Military Romance

Guardian Personal Protection Specialists

Sybil's Protector

Lyra's Protector

Angel Peak Steamy Instalove Novella Series

(Small Town)

By Ellie Masters

EACH BOOK IN THIS SERIES CAN BE READ AS A STANDALONE AND IS ABOUT A DIFFERENT COUPLE WITH AN HEA.

SNOWED IN WITH THE MOUNTAIN DOCTOR

Rescued by the Mountain Guide

Stranded with the Resort Owner

Matched with the Small-Town Chef

Trapped with the Forest Ranger

Snowbound with the Vineyard Owner

Reunited with the Hometown Hero

Colliding with the Coffee Shop Owner

Falling for the Firefighter

Wrecked with the Reclusive Author

Tangled with the Single Dad

Whirlwinded by the Helicopter Pilot

Sheltered by the Veterinarian

Bound by the Sheriff

The One I Want Series

(Small Town, Military Heroes)

By Jet & Ellie Masters

EACH BOOK IN THIS SERIES CAN BE READ AS A STANDALONE
AND IS ABOUT A DIFFERENT COUPLE WITH AN HEA.

Saving Abby

Saving Ariel

Saving Brie

Saving Cate

Saving Dani

Saving Jen

The LaRouge Triplets

Asher

Brody

Cage

Billionaire Romance

Billionaire Boys Club

Hawke

Richard

Contemporary Romance

Cocky Captain

Romantic Suspense

EACH BOOK IS A STANDALONE NOVEL.

The Starling

The Swan

~AND~

Science Fiction

Ellie Masters writing as L.A. Warren

Vendel Rising: a Science Fiction Serialized Novel

———

If you enjoyed this book by Ellie Masters, the LIGHTER SIDE of the Jet & Ellie writing duo, and aren't afraid of edgier writing, you might enjoy reading BDSM themed books written by Jet, the DARKER SIDE of the Masters' Writing Team.

The DARKER SIDE

Jet Masters is the darker side of the Jet & Ellie writing duo!

Romantic Suspense

Changing Roles Series:

THIS SERIES MUST BE READ IN ORDER.

Command Me

Control Me

Collar Me

Embracing FATE

Seizing FATE

Accepting FATE

HOT READS

About the Author

Ellie Masters is a USA Today Bestselling author and Amazon Top 15 Author who writes Angsty, Steamy, Heart-Stopping, Pulse-Pounding, Can't-Stop-Reading Romantic Suspense. In addition, she's a wife, military mom, doctor, and retired Colonel. She writes romantic suspense filled with all your sexy, swoon-worthy alpha men. Her writing will tug at your heartstrings and leave your heart racing.

Born in the South, raised under the Hawaiian sun, Ellie has traveled the globe while in service to her country. The love of her life, her amazing husband, is her number one fan and biggest supporter. And yes! He's read every word she's written.

She has lived all over the United States—east, west, north, south and central—but grew up under the Hawaiian sun. She's also been privileged to have lived overseas, experiencing other cultures and making lifelong friends. Now, Ellie is proud to call herself a Southern transplant, learning to say y'all and "bless her heart" with the best of them.

Ellie's favorite way to spend an evening is curled up on a couch, laptop in place, watching a fire, drinking a good wine, and bringing forth all the characters from her mind to the page and hopefully into the hearts of her readers.

FOR MORE INFORMATION
elliemasters.com

facebook.com/elliemastersromance

x.com/Ellie__Masters

instagram.com/ellie_masters

bookbub.com/authors/ellie-masters

goodreads.com/Ellie_Masters

Connect with Ellie Masters

Website:
elliemasters.com
Purchase Direct:
elliemasters.com/shopify
Amazon Author Page:
elliemasters.com/amazon
Facebook:
elliemasters.com/Facebook
Goodreads:
elliemasters.com/Goodreads
Bookbub:
elliemasters.com/Bookbub
Instagram:
elliemasters.com/Instagram

Final Thoughts

I hope you enjoyed this book as much as I enjoyed writing it. If you enjoyed reading this story, please consider leaving a review on Amazon and Goodreads, and please let other people know. A sentence is all it takes. Friend recommendations are the strongest catalyst for readers' purchase decisions! And I'd love to be able to continue bringing the characters and stories from My-Mind-to-the-Page.

Second, call or e-mail a friend and tell them about this book. If you really want them to read it, gift it to them. If you prefer digital friends, please use the "Recommend" feature of Goodreads to spread the word.

Or visit my blog https://elliemasters.com, where you can find out more about my writing process and personal life.

Come visit The EDGE: Dark Discussions where we'll have a chance to talk about my works, their creation, and maybe what the future has in store for my writing.

Facebook Reader Group: Ellz Bellz

Thank you so much for your support!

Love,

Ellie

DEDICATION

This book is dedicated to you, my reader. Thank you for spending a few hours of your time with me. I wouldn't be able to write without you to cheer me on. Your wonderful words, your support, and your willingness to join me on this journey is a gift beyond measure.

Whether this is the first book of mine you've read, or if you've been with me since the very beginning, thank you for believing in me as I bring these characters 'from my mind to the page and into your hearts.'

Love,
Ellie

THE END

---

www.ingramcontent.com/pod-product-compliance
Lightning Source LLC
Chambersburg PA
CBHW031042310726
48969CB00007B/2080